The
Setup

The Setup

Denise Montgomery

AUGUST 2015

Book Dedication

This book is dedicated to the memory of my mother,
Doris M. Calloway.

To my aunt, Louise Howard. Your kindness and patient is overwhelming. I can't thank you enough for believing in me.

Acknowledgements

Friends are a gift from God. Thank you Freda for your kind words of encouragement, and unwavering friendship.

Elane, Martia, and Sherry. Words are not enough to show my gratitude for the love and kindness that you have shown me throughout the writing of this book.

Mona you are simply the best I can't thank you enough.

For I know the plans I have for you, declares the Lord, plans to prosper you and not to harm you, plans to give you hope and a future."

Jeremiah 29:11

The Setup
By Denise Montgomery

It's a new beginning
It's a new day
Things are turning for me
It's finally going my way
I learned my lesson
Going to do things Gods' way May as well take my time it's all a
Setup anyway.

It was all part of the plan
All part of the game
Twisting turning learning to trust and obey. May as well learn to rest
in his will and his way
Cause it's all just a Setup anyway.

Prologue

Time seemed to stand still as sweat ran down my back in buckets. I heard the car pull up, and the car door slam. It was 2:30 on the dot. I knew I couldn't trust him to come on time. I got the gun off the floor. I gripped it in my hand. Oh my, God, I forgot to load the bullets. There wasn't enough light in the closet to see. Please, God, show me what to do. There were three bullets in the bag. I took out all three. They were very little. I felt the barrel of the gun. I turned it around and managed to open the chamber. The bullets were in my hand. James was surveying the house. Hurry Marie, you don't have much time. I had one bullet in the chamber. Darn it! I dropped one on the floor. Please, Lord, let me get this last bullet in the chamber. The gun was ready. I needed to step out of the closet; if only my hands would stop shaking and my feet start moving.

I watched James as he continued surveying the perimeter of the house. He stepped on the front porch and tried opening the front door. He pushed and pulled on the windows on the porch as well. He moved from the porch to the side of the house. I could shoot myself for not remembering to lock the window when I came through. I needed him to come through the back door.

He tried the first window then the second. He was finally at the third window. He opened it with ease and stepped right in. James was in the house with me. I was sure he heard the pounding of my heart from the closet. I needed him to come a little closer, just a few feet past the door. I didn't want to look him in the eye when I ended his life.

1

In the process of time, all things will work out for the ultimate good. I was seventeen when my life started to unravel. How was I supposed to know that? I had no idea that hard ache, pain and suffering would eventually lead to something better. If somewhere along the way someone could have whispered *don't sweat this it will get better*, my life would have been a lot easier

The Claxton River flooded in the spring of 1990. I was supposed to graduate from high school that year. The river had other plans. The river came knocking and everybody in Claxton Mississippi had to evacuate. Everyone that is except Mama, me and my sister Thelma.

Mama saw the river rising every day just like everybody else. I guess she was waiting for a sign from heaven. We were the only people left on the block. She insisted that things weren't as bad as the news reports were saying. She thought it was just a trick by the city to get everybody to leave. Mama listened to the news and watched the rain coming down, but she refused to leave. She and my sister Thelma kept on praying as the river kept on rising.

Mama finally got the sign she had been waiting on when the water said hello when she stepped out of bed. She heard the frogs and snakes dancing a jig in the front yard. She finally told me and my sister to pack up what few things we had; we were leaving.

We were going to go and live with my Aunt Agnes and Uncle Ralph in Baton Rouge until the water receded. I knew Mama hated the idea of having to go and live with Aunt Agnes. She and her sister were never really close. She said it was because she left Claxton at an early age. Aunt Agnes was left caring for my grandparents all by herself. Anyhow, Aunt Agnes never forgave her for deserting her. Mama did come back, but it wasn't soon enough for Aunt Agnes. She said Aunt Agnes was very selfish and never thought of anyone other than herself.

After Mama came back to Claxton to help with her parents, Aunt Agnes figured it was time to make her escape. She left for school and never returned to Claxton; not even for her own parent's funeral.

Mama remained in the old house that her parents left to both her daughters. But, Aunt Agnes made it clear that she wanted nothing to do with Claxton. She signed over her share to Mama, and that was the end of that.

I guess Mama was lonely. With my grandparents and her only sister gone that had to be the only reason for marrying my Dad.

Dad certainly didn't have a lot of money. He worked as a porter in a hotel in Franklin. Franklin is just over the bridge from Claxton.

Mama and Daddy continued to live in my grandparent's house. They had their share of problems; with no money being the biggest. Times were tough. Mama found a few odd jobs around town to make ends meet.

It was after a few years in the house that she gave birth to my sister Thelma. Common sense should have kicked in and told her that one child was enough, but no she nagged Daddy about having another child. She thought having another child would bring them closer together. She told him it was a good idea to have children close in age.

My Daddy insisted there would be no more children. Lots of good that did Mama had her own idea. She got pregnant again. That's how I came along. She told him that I was an accident. Mama thought that would smooth things over with him. Boy was she wrong. After I was born, the marriage was pretty much over. Daddy hung around I guess because he didn't have any other place to go.

When I was ten and Thelma was twelve, we came home from school one evening. Mama was crying. She said Daddy was gone. I was never to bring up the subject of my father again. I've never been the type just to accept things without question. I had to know where my Daddy was.

I ran into the kitchen one evening after school, "Mama where did my Daddy go?"

Mama looked at me with fire in her eyes, "He's gone Marie I already told you that. Your father is not coming back. You are not to speak about him to me again. Do you understand?"

Telling me no, was like saying go out and hire a private investigator. I couldn't rest until I knew the truth.

All I had to do was ask around to a few of our noisy neighbors that pretended to be Mama's friends.

The gossip around town was he had skipped town with some woman he met in a bar. The way I see it good riddance to the both of them. After that I never asked about him again.

Having been born and raised in this god forsaken mosquito ridden hole in the wall. The flood was an answer to my prayer. I was finally getting out of this place. We left Claxton on a Friday morning around ten. I got up that morning at seven and stood in the front yard water around my ankles. I prayed that the good Lord would let the water wash the house out to sea. I was so caught up I didn't hear Mama calling my name.

"Marie are you gonna stay out there all morning? Or maybe you could help me and your sister pack the rest of our things." It didn't make sense to me anyhow why Mama continued to stay in Claxton after her parents died.

It wasn't because they left her some great big fortune that she had to stay and protect. My aunt was smart she left on the first thing smoking as soon as she had a chance. She left Mama with this run down house close to the river. Along with five acres of land way out in the country. She didn't have the faintest idea what she was going to do with; it wasn't like she was a farmer about to plant her first crop.

Before we left for Baton Rouge, Mama had to take a leave of absence from her job with the Larson family. She had worked for them white folks all my life. They didn't even offer to help Mama get a place when they found out she had to move. Told her not to worry her job would be here when she returned.

The Friday morning we were leaving, Mama and Thelma did everything imaginable to delay the inevitable. When I just couldn't take it any longer, I ran to the side of the house and screamed, "Oh my God, there are snakes all over the back yard!" I don't believe I have ever seen Thelma move that fast, she could have run the last lap of a relay race, she definitely would have won.

We loaded the car and drove out the yard. We were finally on our way to Baton Rouge. I prayed it would be a permanent move. The look on Mama and Thelma face's said they would need CPR at any minute.

We were just about to the main highway when Mama stopped the car. She and Thelma started praying, *Lord, please protect my house. Please don't let any hurt, harm, or danger come near my dwelling.* I believe Mama and Thelma called every angel in heaven to watch over the place. While I sat in the back seat and prayed that God was busy and didn't hear a word.

Leaving Claxton was the best thing that had ever happened to me. I had lived here all of my life. I could not think of one positive thing that had happened in my life while living here. As I looked out the back window of the car, I decided right then and there that I wasn't coming back, but then I thought about it. Just in case Mama made me come back. Claxton definitely wouldn't be my final stop.

We arrived in Baton Rouge at night. It was breathtaking to look at the lights shining on the water. My aunt and uncle were expecting our arrival. Mama considered Uncle Ralph and Aunt Agnes well off because they lived in a four bedroom house. Aunt Agnes put me and Thelma together in one bedroom, and Mama in another bedroom.

My cousins, Michael, and Chaz were fit to be tied when they found out that one of them would have to move in with the other during our visit. They made sure we knew they weren't happy with the arrangement.

Living with my aunt and uncle was alright. It was nice living in that big old house instead of that two bedroom shack in Claxton.

Mama checked the news station every day for any word on the flooding in Mississippi. Every day the word was the same the flood-waters were slowly receding, but not enough for residents to return home. I begged and begged her to look for a place for us to stay in Baton Rouge, but she insisted that Claxton was our home and rest assured we were going back.

Aunt Agnes was no help at all. I could tell she couldn't wait to get her baby sister and her two girls out of her house. We were a reminder of all that she left behind in Claxton.

I don't think our presence seemed to bother Uncle Ralph all that much, as long as he had his cigars and his TV. Life was good.

My aunt and uncle married right out college and have been to-gether ever since. They met in Baton Rouge when my aunt left Claxton. After moving to Baton Rouge, she went on to finish her col-lege degree. She found a good job and later met Uncle Ralph. I never knew for the life of me why Mama didn't get the hint and follow along.

Baton Rouge was everything Claxton was not. There were people, places and things to do all the time. Mama warned me not to get too comfortable she could tell Baton Rouge was growing on me.

She made sure I understood we would be heading back home as soon the city was declared safe.

Mama was so protective of my sister and I. Folks could not believe that I was eighteen and Thelma was twenty. She kept a tight rein on us after my Daddy left us for that other woman. Thelma never thought about leaving, leaving was constantly on my mind. Every time I would try to talk to her about leaving, she would give me the same old speech, "You girls are all that I have since your Daddy left me.

I know some day you will have to leave me, but you don't have to be in no hurry." Then she would look like she was about to burst into tears at any moment. It worked every time. Thelma and I would drop any idea of leaving.

I don't think Mama's protective nature bothered Thelma. She and Mama were like two peas in a pod. She did everything Mama asked her. Not me, I made up my mind that I would get a taste of freedom even if it was for only a little while. I figured we would be in Baton Rouge at least two weeks. That had meant two weeks of freedom before I had to go back.

I wanted to go out and have a little fun. With Thelma being older than me; I knew if I wanted to get out of the house I would need to drag her along. Since she and I were exact opposites, that would be hard to do. She hated everything about Baton Rouge. She was hoping and praying that we go home every day. I knew if I told that goodie two shoes that I wanted to go out that she would go right back and tell Mama.

After we had been in Baton Rouge for a week, I overheard my cousins talking about a party that was happening in the house on the next street. The parents of the kid that lived there would be away for the evening. He was planning on having a few kids over. My cousins couldn't wait to get away from their parents, so I didn't have to worry about them shooting off their mouth to anyone. The only problem was Thelma. Mama made sure that I never left the house without my big sister. I knew there was absolutely no way I would talk Thelma into taking me. I was on my own. My cousins had no intention of letting me tag along with them. There was no way I was going to miss that party. I would just have to sneak out the house.

I waited until the lights were out, and I eased out of bed. I was already fully dressed. I managed to get under the covers before Thelma could see me. I made it down the stairs and out the back door. I was on my way. The house was only one block over. I figured the lights would be on, so it wouldn't be a problem finding the house.

The party was in full swing when I arrived. Stepping into that party was like walking into another world. I totally forgot about Mama, Thelma, or Claxton. I had never seen anything like this. The house was beautiful, with a large pool in the back. Kids were dancing and drinking.

The boys at the party were nothing like the boys in Claxton. These boys could put words together to make a sentence. They were paying attention to me; Marie Rhodes from Claxton Mississippi. I never wanted this to end. I guess that's the reason I didn't realize it was after 1:00 in the morning. I grabbed my coat to make may exit, but it was too late. The neighbors called the police, they were knocking on the door. They took all the kids out into the front yard. By this time, the entire neighborhood was awake. Angry parents were storming toward the front yard from every direction.

The next thing I knew my aunt and uncle and of course Mama and Thelma were coming to drag me away. I wanted to remind them that I was eighteen years old, but it didn't seem right at the time.

Of course I never thought I would live it down; they went on for hours and hours about all the sins I had committed, and I should be more careful.

Well, one thing for sure that party made me even more determined to get out of Claxton and get Mama and Thelma out of my life.

The next morning Mama informed my aunt and uncle that we were going back to Claxton. We would just have to live in a motel in town if the house were uninhabitable. She said that Baton Rouge was a bad influence on her daughters, and she needed to get us home.

We packed up all our belonging and left for Claxton. I sat in the back seat like a puppy looking out the window. I tasted the salt of my tears for hours as the buildings of Baton Rouge faded in the distance. Of course Mama and Thelma were overjoyed; they were taking me back home where I would be safe and protected.

2

When we got back to Claxton our old house on Murray Lane was still standing, but it was a total mess. There was mud, bugs, and mildew everywhere. It smelled like all the fish in the river swam through the front door and died.

Mama was devastated. She and Thelma cried and prayed all afternoon. After they had finished praying, they tried their best to think of a way for us to move back into that deserted river bed.

I wanted no part of that house. I turned on my heels and got back in the car. After a while, it finally dawned on Mama that we couldn't stay there any longer.

Mama called around to all her church-going friends to see if we could stay with them for a while. Every call was the same, "I'm sorry Sister Margaret we will keep you in prayer, but we are all in the same shape as you folks."

Mama had no choice but to call Mrs. Larson, the old white lady she worked for. Her employer for most of her life. She told her that we could move into the small two bedroom guest house in back of the main house. I hated the idea. *I wanted no part of living behind the big house.* It was bad enough Mama worked her fingers to the bone for this old lady. Now we have to go and move on the property.

We drove over to the Larson's house. Before I could open the car door to get out Mama grabbed my arm, "Marie please, be on your best behavior. I need you to shut up and be grateful that we have some place to live until we can find a place of our own." I pretended like I was listening and hurried out of the car. I knew how important it was for Mama to keep up appearances with Mrs. Larson, so I made peace with the move and tried my best to smile when she rang the front door bell.

Mrs. Larson finally opened the door. She took one look at us and told us to walk around the side of the house to the guest house. I wanted to scream. We could easily have gone through the main house to get to the guest house, but we had to be reminded we were the hired help.

Mrs. Larson gave Mama one day to get settled in the guest house; then she was right back to work. Thelma resumed her nursing studies at the junior college downtown.

I finally received my high school diploma in the mail. I took that degree and went into town and found myself a job at the only department store in Claxton. Mama wanted me to go to school with Thelma, but school was the last thing on my mind.

I worked thirty hours a week at the store. I knew I needed to look for something better, but it did not seem to matter.

On days when I finished early I would feel sorry for Mama and go by the house and help her finish her work. The old girl wasn't getting any younger. Mrs. Larson still expected her to clean that big house with the speed she had years ago.

I hated the fact that she never took the time to try and learn a skill. I wanted her to quit working for this old white woman. Mama settled for anything after Daddy left her. I hated him for what he put her through.

Working with Mama gave me an opportunity to see how people were supposed to live. The Larson's house was a grand old estate home. I often wondered if it had been a slave plantation. It wouldn't be too much of a stretch of the imagination to find out the Larson's ancestor's had owned slaves.

One afternoon while Mama cleaned upstairs I sat in the formal dining room and pretended that I was having a big fancy dinner party, all the important people in town were there. I got so caught up in my day dreaming I didn't realize Mama was standing in the door watching me. She waited until I turned around and realized she was standing there. She dusted her way around to my side of the table.

She asked me to move closer to her for a minute. I could feel a speech coming on.

"Sweetheart you were really caught up in your pretending. Marie, I worry about you so much more that your sister. If you would only accept the life you have and try to make it better, life would be so much easier for you. Marie, you don't have to covet what other people have. Sweetheart coveting is a sin."

I wanted to explode. It took every ounce of control in me not to go off on her, but I still couldn't bring myself to hurt her when I knew she meant well. Mama didn't know any better. I took a deep breath and got up from the table. I should have just walked out. I knew Mama would never change, but I just couldn't.

I turned around and looked right in her eyes, "Mama the only sin here is that you don't realize that you could own this house and that is a sin and shame."

Mama got up from the chair and pretended to dust the large cabinet on the wall. In her low muffled voice, "I did the best I could with what I had after your Daddy left us for that other women. Being a maid was the only job I could find with a tenth- grade education and two kids to feed. I'm sorry I couldn't give you all the things that you think you deserve Marie. I hope one day you will understand that I did the best I could."

I wasn't in the mood for Mama's pity party. I got up walked over to her and kissed her cheek. I politely walked out the front door of the big house.

3

Mama and I never got along all that well, but our relationship was at least cordial. After the afternoon at the Larson's things were never quite the same.

We continued to live in the guest house for two more years. Mama never gave up the idea of moving back to the old house on Murray Lane. She would drive by the old neighborhood and check on the house every chance she got. A few people came back now and then. They tried to make repairs to their property, but the neighborhood was never the same.

The city finally built a levee to protect the remaining houses in the area. The levee only made her more determined to go back. If she'd had the money to fix up that old house that's what she would have done. In her heart that would always be home. She would move back into her mother's house.

Mama finally broke down and found a small house to rent about 20 minutes from the old house. The new house had three bedrooms. I was finally going to get a room of my own. It was the first time in my life I didn't have to share a bedroom with my older sister.

Thelma was in her last semester of nursing school. We were all excited about her upcoming graduation pending the passing of her exam. She had already secured a job at the new hospital in Franklin. I tried to convince her to get herself a car. She told me she would give the idea some thought, but she didn't think that would be a good idea right now with Mama having to adjust to a new house.

Thelma and I were never close. For some reason, we never bonded like most sisters do. She never had that much to say to me other than to relate orders from Mama. We never had sisterly conversations or did things that I imagined most sisters did.

One evening Thelma and I were in the kitchen finishing the dishes. She asked me if I was dating anyone, and of course I told her no. I had no intention of giving her any information to take back to Mama. It felt strange talking to my sister this way. She asked me to sit down at the table with her. I wanted to leave. She leaned in close to me, as if she was about to leak secret messages from the government.

"Marie can you keep a secret? I'm not ready to tell Mama just yet."

I didn't know what to think, I thought maybe she decided to change her hairstyle, and she didn't want her to know. For the life of me I couldn't think of anything that would be so important that Thelma would be telling me instead of Mama. I braced myself and sat back in the chair for this bombshell that she was about to unload.

She spoke in a hushed voice, "Marie you have to promise you won't say a word to Mama until I have graduated, do you promise?"

I was becoming annoyed with this cat and mouse game, but I went along with it because it's not like I talk to my sister every day. To reassure her that I wouldn't tell Mama, I reached over and touched her hand and looked her in her eyes, "I promise Thelma, you can trust me."

"Marie I have met the most awesome man in the world. He is a 3rd year resident at the hospital. His father is the chief surgeon. He and I started talking about six months ago. He has asked me out on several occasions, and I'm finding it hard to say no. I think I would like to go, but I am terrified. I don't want to make a mistake and take things too fast. What do you think I should do Marie?"

God help me I tried my best to look serious. I needed to remember that this was my older sister who was sitting across from me, trying to figure out if she should go out on a freaking date with a doctor for heaven's sake. I wanted to scream.

"Thelma you did say he was a doctor, and his father is a surgeon. I did get that part right?"

"Yes, Marie he is a doctor, but that doesn't matter to me."

I had to keep reminding myself that this dumb girl sitting across from me was in fact, my sister. But it was getting increasingly harder to concentrate when all I could think about was this is my way out of Claxton. I didn't know how I was going to pull it off, but one thing for sure the good doctor would be my ticket out of Claxton.

I continued to listen as Thelma went on and on about what Mama would say when she found out. She didn't want to disappoint Mama because she had promised her she would finish school before she started seeing anyone.

When she realized that I wasn't listening she asked me if everything was alright. I gave her some excuse about being tired and told her to wait until after graduation and invite the young man over for dinner.

I assured her that Mama would be okay with the idea once she met the doctor. I told her to stop worrying; it wasn't like they were getting married next week. That seemed to ease her fears for a little while.

It was hard to believe that Thelma was terrified to tell her that she had found a nice guy that she was interested in dating. When I stopped to give the matter some thought; it was even worst that her mother wouldn't be happy with her.

For once in her life Thelma took my advice. She secretly dated the doctor. They would meet after work, or before he went on rounds at the hospital. There was even a change in her attitude toward me. She would wait until Mama was asleep and come into my room at night to tell me all about her day at the hospital. Her face would light up like a Christmas tree when she mentioned CJ. He preferred to be called CJ, which was short for Charles Jamison. I was eager to hear everything there was to him. I needed to know every detail about his life and his family; these details were all being woven into my plan.

Thelma and I continued to exchange secret glances when Mama wasn't looking. She was a glowing light every time we got together for our secret talks. It was nice to see my sister so happy for the first time in her life.

She finished school and her training at the hospital. The only thing that remained was graduation and the final exam.

At the end of the semester, she took the test for her nurse's license. Of course, she passed it with flying colors. She started working at the hospital. Mama was so proud of her.

Thelma came in one evening and showed Mama a picture of her in her cap and gown. She cried and carried on for hours. From then on she took that picture with her everywhere. I believe everybody at church had seen it at least a hundred times.

4

Thelma's graduation was finally here. I wanted Mama to look extra special, so I purchased her a new dress from the store. The dress was laid out on her bed when she came in from work. She looked it over and told me how pretty it was, but I needed to take it back to the store. Mrs. Larson had given her one of her dresses to wear.

"Marie this dress is far too fancy for me, and it must have cost you a small fortune."

I didn't want Mama to know how disappointed I was that she would rather wear an old hand-me-down than to wear a new dress for her daughter's graduation. I practically had to threaten her to get her to try the dress on. It was only after Thelma, and I insisted that she agreed to wear it.

The graduation was at 3:00 on a Saturday afternoon. I made sure Mama didn't answer the phone. I knew it would be just like that old witch, Mrs. Larson to call her in on her off day.

We arrived at the school auditorium an hour before the start of the program. Mama wanted to make sure she got a good seat right down front. She wanted to be sure she saw Thelma when she crossed the stage to accept her degree.

The Dean of students began calling names. "Tammy Faye Rhimes, Thelma Diane Rhoades." It was all I could do to catch Mama before she went over the railing. She was so proud of Thelma. She held her graduation picture in her hand and hugged it close to her heart. I would have given anything to keep her as happy as she was at that very moment. When the ceremony was over, we all walked outside to wait for Thelma. Mama chatted with a few other parents who had children graduating. If she showed that graduation picture to one person she showed it to a hundred.

I was tired and ready to get out of my shoes. My feet were killing me. I walked ahead of her to lean against the building.

Mama looked over at me every two to three minutes to make sure I was alive. She reminded me that she had a feast fit for a king waiting for us at the house, as if that would make my feet stop hurting.

Thelma finally emerged from the crowd. She was smiling from ear to ear. It didn't take long for me to figure out she wasn't just smiling about her new degree. Attached to her hip was the most gorgeous hunk of a man that I had ever seen. He was a cool glass of water that I wanted to drink.

I was still in total shock when CJ, aka Dr. Morrison, extended his right hand toward Mama. Thelma introduced him, "Mama this is Dr. Charles Morrison Jr., but he likes to be called CJ. He is a 3rd year resident at the hospital."

All the blood in Mama's face was gone. I was sure her heart had stopped beating. She never said a word. She turned and looked at me with her *I am ready to go look*. I stood perfectly still I had no intention of leaving until I met Dr. Charles Morrison Jr.

Thelma realized that I was waiting to be introduced, so she walked the doctor toward me. Before she could say, this is my sis, "Hello my name is Marie. I'm Thelma's younger sister. You must be CJ I have heard so much about you. But Thelma's description of you did not do you justice at all.

Thelma and the doctor turned to locate Mama who was half way to the car. Thelma caught up with her and told her that CJ and his parents had made reservations for us at a restaurant downtown.

I was giddy with excitement I totally forgot that my feet were on fire. I walked over to the car toward Mama. She was dying. I was sure she would need the paramedics at any minute. Mama pulled Thelma's arm and walked off. She tried to whisper, but anger was getting the best of her.

"Thelma I don't need dinner with your friend the doctor. I have enough food cooked at home to feed an army. Why on earth did you let me walk into this trap?"

Thelma tried to remain calm, but I could tell panic and embarrassment were taking control. She stood between the doctor and Mama wondering what on earth she should do.

I guess I could have been more of a supportive sister, but at the time I really couldn't focus clearly. Dr. Gorgeous had taken my breath away. Besides I didn't understand why Mama was in such a tizzy.

Mama and Thelma continued to stand near her old car and argue.

The doctor didn't quite know what to do. So being the Good Samaritan that I am I walked over grabbed his hand, "Is your car near here or did you park in the rear of the auditorium?"

"No, my car is right over here. I planned to drive everyone to the restaurant. But it doesn't look like your mom is going to go for that idea."

"Which car did you say was yours?"

"It's the blue one over there."

I turned in the direction that he was pointing. My eyes lit up like a burning building. The only blue car in that direction was a brand new Cadillac.

In my loudest voice I yelled in their direction, "I'm getting hungry are you guys coming or should I go on to the restaurant with CJ?"

Thelma continued to plead her case, "Mama won't you at least come to the restaurant and meet CJ, I mean Dr. Morrison before you make up your mind about him?"

Mama looked like she was ready for her burial, but she finally surrendered and agreed that she would only go to the restaurant for a few minutes, and only if she could drive her car.

Thelma explained that she would rather that we all ride together with CJ to save having to pay two parking fees. Whenever the subject of money is brought up with Mama, it doesn't take too much convincing to change her mind.

CJ walked ahead of us and pulled the car up closer, so she wouldn't have to walk that far. He got out of the car and walked over to open the car door for Thelma and Mama. I got in on the other side. Mama was quite uncomfortable. She didn't want any part of this dinner.

Thelma sat in the front seat as far away from CJ as she possibly could. At one point I was sure she was a statue, her head never moved, and she never once glanced over the seat to check on Mama.

Mama didn't say one single solitary word during the drive downtown. She was praying. I knew that from the constant rocking back and forth. I felt so sorry for Thelma; and Mama as well it seemed they both didn't realize that we had been given a gift. CJ was the answer to all of our problems. I knew for sure that he would ask Thelma to marry him in time.

Any man that could put up with Thelma for any length of time had to be genuinely interested. One thing for sure when Thelma married him there was no way she would leave Mama in that old rent house. Of course, that meant that I would be leaving as well. You can bet I won't be leaving empty-handed. If Thelma didn't have sense enough to cash in on this meal ticket I sure as heck planned too.

The blue Cadillac rode like a dream. I have never in my life ridden in a car like this. The interior of the car was blue leather. It was soft and smooth as a newborn baby. I couldn't help but wonder if he was making enough money to afford a car like this or did his daddy get it for him? I figured Mama was already upset so why not get all the information I could, "Dr. Morrison I mean CJ this is truly an exquisite car, have you had it long?"

"As a matter of fact I've only had it for a couple of months it was a gift from my dad, for finishing my residency.

"Oh, I see you have finished all your classes, and you are in your residency program? Just what does that mean? Will you be opening a practice or what?" I dared not look at Mama I'm sure by now she wanted to push me out of the moving car.

"Well I will be finished in a few more months, and then I can practice medicine. But I'm still thinking about a specialty?" I was just about to ask what specialty when the two of them gave me the death stare. I decided I would let the questions go for the time being and enjoy the ride. I knew there would be plenty of time for me to find out all I need to know about Dr. Charles Jamison Morrison Jr.

5

The car was a tomb until we pulled into the parking lot of the most expensive restaurant I've ever seen. It was in the upscale end of town. You can be for sure the folks in my neighborhood didn't eat here on a regular basis. The parking lot was crowded with all types of expensive cars.

CJ jumped out of the car and ran to the other side to open the door for Thelma and Mama. Before he could grab the car door, Mama was out and waiting.

I thought I had died and gone to heaven when I walked into that restaurant. There were waiters in white jackets and linen napkins on the tables. The only linen napkins I had ever seen belonged to the Larson's.

The Maitre'D greeted CJ by name. I was impressed. He led us to our table. Already seated at the table were two other people. I assumed these were the good doctor's parents. His father stood when we arrived at the table and extended his hand toward Mama. Of course mother didn't return the gesture.

CJ introduced Mama first, then me. It appeared that his parents were already familiar with Thelma. Mama didn't smile, grunt, or moo; she just sat down and looked totally uncomfortable.

The waiter came over to get our drink orders. When he got to Mama, she managed to get our water like a dying person on a dessert. I wanted so badly to try a mixed drink, but I knew I wouldn't live to get it down my throat. I ordered tea instead. Mama could hardly stand it when CJ's parents ordered drinks from the bar. Thelma tried her best to make things easier for, but I don't think that was possible. After an hour of aimless chatter, Mama couldn't take it any longer. She asked me to go to the ladies room with her. I pretended like I didn't hear her until she nearly yanked my arm out of the socket. I got up and followed her to the restroom. I looked back at Thelma who looked like she was on the verge of tears.

The restrooms were beautiful. Mama of course, was very uncomfortable being in the restroom with other white women. She waited until the women left before she said a word, "Marie I am ready to go. I don't want to be here any longer; we don't belong here."

"Mama, you have worked hard all of your life. Don't you think it's time that you enjoyed being pampered for a change? Why can't you just enjoy yourself, this is not costing you a dime."

"I don't believe I asked for your opinion just your help. Now when we get back out there you are going to say that you have to get home, you have to go into work."

"So Mama you are asking me to lie for you." I responded with a sly smile.

"It's not a lie Marie when you are helping your mother. Now do as I say and help me get out of this restaurant, I'm ready to get home and get out of this dress and eat my dinner."

"Mama, I am not ready to leave, so if you want to go you will have to speak up for yourself." I said the words, but I couldn't believe they were coming out of my mouth. I turned and looked at Mama. She was about to explode. She turned and hurried out of the ladies room.

When we got back to the table Thelma looked up in relief, "Is everything alright, you were in the ladies room for such a long time?" I was about to speak when Mama broke in…

"Yes everything is fine, it's just that Marie forgot that she has to go into work this evening, and we should be going." Mama jumped up from her seat and headed toward the door. CJ"s parents rose to say goodbye, but it was too late she was already at the exit. I turned and said my goodbyes to the doctor's parents and told Thelma that we would be waiting outside for her.

Mama was fit to be tied as she stood by the blue Cadillac. Finally, CJ Thelma, and his parents emerged. They walked over to the car. "Mrs. Rhodes it was so nice meeting you. I hope we get the chance to have dinner together another time. Thelma is a lovely girl, and she makes our son quite happy."

Mama was speechless. All of her suspicions had just been proven. She turned and pulled on the door of the car when it wouldn't open she yelled at CJ, "Would you please open this door I would like to go home!"

I sat in the back seat with Mama; I felt so bad for Thelma. What could be wrong with finding a nice young man that cared about you? It was so obvious that the doctor genuinely cared for Thelma.

We arrived back at the auditorium to get our car. I think Mama was out of the car even before it came to a complete stop. I got out on my side and walked around to CJ, "It was nice meeting you. Please forgive my mother's behavior she is just not ready to let go of her girls, but please don't let this run you off."

I looked over at Thelma and gave her a smile, "Hang in there sis you knew it would be tough, but she will come around."

Mama was in the car and waiting for me to get in. I guess it was taking me too long before I knew it she was driving straight for me. I have never seen her drive like that. She stopped the car inches from my feet. She yelled out the window, "Are you getting in or will you be walking home?" I opened the car door, and I don't even remember sitting down before Mama was taking off. She pulled up to the side of CJ's car and yelled, "Thelma Diane Rhodes I am ready to go home, and you are riding home with your family!"

Thelma turned to take a final look at CJ and quietly got out of the car. She walked over to the car and got in. She waved at CJ like a child waving out the school bus window on the first day of school.

There was no use trying to talk to her when she was like this. Neither of us said a word as she drove like a mad woman down the freeway to our house.

When we got home, she went straight to the kitchen. She told Thelma to follow her. I continued to walk toward the kitchen behind Thelma. When she saw that I was coming as well, she turned to me, "Marie this is between me and Thelma I don't need you in here right now."

6

Thelma

I Couldn't believe Mama's behavior today. I knew she would be shocked, but nothing like this. I turned to Marie and smiled. For the first time in my life, I had to tell Mama what I wanted. I looked at her and then to Marie. "Mama it won't be necessary for Marie to leave, she should know what's going on. I want her to stay, sit down Marie."

It's hard to believe that even as a grown woman I found it intimidating to speak with my mother about my feeling. I knew at that moment Mama wanted to object, but she didn't say a word. She gathered her composure as she looked me square in the eye, she was ready for a fight. I was ready as well. Before she could say a word I spoke up, "Mama I love you, and I have always respected and followed all the advice that you have given me. Mama you asked me not to get involved with anyone before I graduated, and I didn't. Charles and I have known each other for over two years. I told him that I couldn't see anyone until after I graduated, and he agreed to wait because he was busy with his studies, and he respected my wishes. But Mama it's time now. I like Charles, and I would like to see where this could go. Mama, I will be seeing a lot more of him, and we would like your blessing. He is a wonderful man. You just have to get to know him.

Mama looked at me, "I just have one question since you are telling me what your plans are. When you answer, please be honest."

"Okay, Mama you can ask me anything, and I will answer as truthfully as I can."

"Well, Thelma you are a beautiful girl. Any man would be happy to have you. I don't understand how this rich doctor would pick such a common girl from a poor family when he could pick any of them pretty rich doctors walking around the hospital. So, Thelma tell me are you sleeping with him?"

I had to admit I didn't see that one coming. I took a quick glance at Marie for some reaction or the slightest response. We both were on pins and needles as I prayed for the right words to say.

"Mama how could you even ask me that, of course, I haven't slept with him. I told him I won't sleep with a man that I'm not married to."

CJ cares for me, Mama. He is willing to wait until after we're married. I have never met a man like him. He is kind and generous, and thoughtful of my feelings. He makes me feel like I can do anything.

The stress of the evening was beginning to take its toll on Mama; she began rubbing her head and her eyes as tears began to stream down her face. "Thelma you know that I am very proud of you, but I just think you need to give this some time. You just graduated, you're starting a new job, and you have a lot more responsibility. I can't believe the first guy you are seriously interested in is a doctor at the hospital where you just happen to work. What will everybody think of you? You don't want your name to be trashed around the hospital. Thelma I just don't want you to be hurt."

"You don't have to worry about that Mama; we are very careful."

Mama wouldn't give up without a fight. She continued to make her case against CJ, but this was much too important to me. I couldn't allow her to have the last word. I watched Marie as she watched the interaction between Mama and me. For once I could tell my little sister was finally proud of her big sister. CJ was the best thing that had ever happened to me. I couldn't let her mess this up for me. We continued talking in the kitchen for a while longer. It was apparent Mama was losing steam. I won the battle, but the war was not over. I had taken the first step to controlling my life.

Mama was tough. She began watching me like a hawk on a chicken.

She wouldn't budge an inch. She wanted to know where I was, who I was with, and who else would be there whenever I left the house. All the watching and checking in on me didn't bother me one bit. As long as I could see CJ nothing else mattered.

Time passed. I began to see more and more of him. He asked Mama to call him CJ, but she refused. It would always be Dr. Morrison. I guess saying that would mean she was finally accepting the fact that we were a couple.

CJ was doing everything he could to win her over. When he would come to visit me, he would always bring her a gift. I told him that she loved pastries from a bakery downtown. He would make it a point to stop by and get her a treat before he would come to the house.

There were a few times I thought he was getting through to her that he cared about me. But she stayed true to form. If she cared anything about him, she would never let me or anyone else know. I was determined not to allow her to come between us. CJ was my future. I knew that the first time I laid eyes on him.

CJ's residency was over a few months after my graduation. He chose surgery as his specialty which meant more years of training. He and I were both working long hours, which made the time we spent together even more special. We grew closer and closer with every minute we spent together.

It was becoming increasingly harder to keep our relationship a secret. It didn't help that every unmarried nurse in the hospital had their eye on him. I wanted to scratch their eyes out, every time I saw one of them making a play for his attention. I longed for the day when I could tell them that he belongs to me.

CJ was always full of surprises. He loved bringing me little gifts from the strangest places. But, his behavior for the past two weeks was becoming even more bazaar. He started asking me questions about the type of jewelry I liked? What was my favorite vacation spot? I wanted to tell him that going across the state line would be a vacation for me. The only place I had been in my entire life was to Baton Rouge when the house flooded.

One evening after work, he took me out to dinner. After we finished, eating we went on a drive down by the river. We looked at old estate homes. He asked me if I had a choice what type of home I would like to live in someday. I wondered did he know I would live in a tent under the bridge as long as he was there with me. I finally figured out that the strange behavior was leading up to a marriage proposal. I could feel it, I knew he was going to ask me to marry him. I looked over at this gorgeous man and thanked God for allowing him to love me. There was only one problem. I couldn't possibly leave Mama and Marie in their present condition. I just couldn't move to the other side of town in the lap of luxury while they lived in a run-down rent house. How could I make CJ understand that I had to take Mama and Marie with me? It would only be a matter of time for Marie, and she would be leaving. But I knew we would have Mama for the rest of our lives.

It would be ideal if we could fix the old house on Murray. I know that's where she wanted to live.

Marie would have to move back to the house as well, so that ends that idea. I know for sure there wasn't a chance of that happening.

"Hey sweetheart where did you go? You look like you were a thousand miles away. Is everything Okay? I hope you're not worried about your mother are you? Thelma, I won't stop until I have won your mother over. Even if it takes the rest of our lives."

We continued driving in the cool night air. I never wanted this night to end. We drove until we were out in the country. The stars were gleaming in the sky as the moon peeked in and out of the clouds. CJ stopped the car on the side of the road in front of an old white picket fence.

We got out of the car and walked over to the gate. We gazed at the stars. I was so caught up in the stars that I hadn't noticed CJ was kneeling on the ground.

He took my hand, Thelma I can't imagine life without you. I want to spend the rest of my life making you happy. Thelma will you marry."

"Yes! Yes! I can't wait to be your wife!"

CJ reached into the pocket of his jacket and pulled out a little black box. I knew he could hear my heart beating. When he opened the box, I thought the moon had left the sky. It was the most beautiful shiny diamond I had ever seen. He placed the ring on my left hand. It was far too big, but I didn't care I never wanted to take it off. "CJ I love it and

I love you."

"The ring belonged to my grandmother. I know she would be so excited if she knew you were wearing it. I'll have it sized I can't wait until everyone knows you are going to be my wife. I love you Thelma Rhoades."

7

Marie

Thelma continued to work at the hospital, and I continued to work at the store. With all the attention Mama was focusing on Thelma, she hardly had any time to nosy into my business. I turned twenty-two that summer. I finally felt like I could do as I pleased. I saved up enough money to get myself a car. It wasn't much to look at, but it was mine, and that car spelled freedom away from all the drama with Thelma and Mama.

I bought it from a guy in the newspaper. Mama was sure I got a bad deal. It didn't matter to me what I paid for the car. There was no need for me to continue to work in Claxton. I started looking for work in Franklin. I found a job at Wilson's Fine Clothing. After six months, I was promoted to head sales clerk in the Ladies Wear Department. I loved every minute of the thirty-minute drive to work. I loved working at the department store, with all the new clothes and shoes coming in every week. When I got paid every other week, I would hit the sale rack. Pretty soon, my closet looked like a bargain basement.

Of course Mama hated it. She said it was, "Just sinful for one person to own all those clothes when there were so many people in need." That wasn't my problem. I knew I would need all those clothes when I finally left Claxton.

I wanted to celebrate my 22nd birthday in grand form. I decided it was time I visited my first-night club. I didn't want to go to a club in Claxton. It wouldn't do for one of Mama's church going friends to see me in a club that they had no business in as well. I told Mama that I was working late in the store, so I would probably stay in town at my friend Cathy's apartment. Cathy was also a new sales clerk at the same place. She worked in the shoe department. We started talking in the break room one day at lunch. Within days, it was as if we had been friends forever. Cathy was new to town. She had a one bedroom apartment in Franklin not too far from the store. Mama didn't like the idea of me spending time with her. She thought it was sinful for a young girl to live on her own in an apartment away from the safety of her parents. I listened to her fuss for a while before I told her I had to go back to work. One part of the story was correct.

I would be going to work at some point after I went out with Cathy. The other part of the story was a lie. I had no intention of spending the night at her apartment. It was time I started living life.

If I met a nice guy that I wanted to spend some time with what was wrong with that?

We got off work at 6:00. We went back to her apartment and changed clothes before we headed over to the club for Happy Hour. I would finally get to wear my new mini skirt with my new leather boots. I was dying to wear that outfit.

My hair was very flat and limp. Most of the time, I kept it up in a ponytail. There wasn't much else I could do with it. At least I had length going for me. It was below my shoulders. When I wore it down it did look half way decent.

Cathy and I looked wild and sexy when we walked out the apartment that evening. We had the night planned out. Who ever met a guy first would let the other one know if they were planning on leaving with him. Cathy has been to this place a few times. She knew all the regular guys that hung out at Happy Hour.

I stepped into the club like I had a million dollars in my pockets. I knew I looked good. Cathy helped me with my makeup. My big brown eyes popped and sparkled. My skin glowed and my lips were like freshly bloomed roses.

I loved the atmosphere in the club. It felt like I was back in the party in Baton Rouge. This is where I belonged. After I danced until my legs hurt, I noticed that Cathy had secured us a table. I was so ready to sit down. When I reached my seat, the waitress brought over a drink.

I didn't want to be rude, but I hadn't ordered anything. I whispered to the waitress, "Excuse me ma'am but I didn't order this."

"No ma'am the tall gentleman at the bar told me to bring it over."

I looked over at Cathy with fear in my eyes, "Cathy what do I do? I don't know this guy and he is sending me a drink."

"Well for starters you could tell the waitress to tell him thank you. Then he will know you're interested."

"Waitress which gentleman did you say sent the drink over."

She whispered, "The tall gentleman leaning against the bar the good looking guy with the hat on."

I glanced in the direction of the bar, trying to appear not too interested. Quite by surprise, my eyes caught a glimpse of a tall chocolate colored piece of heaven smiling at me. My heart was pounding in my chest. Cathy was practically screaming in my ears, "Say thank you!" With glass in hand I smiled and nodded my head to thank him.

I took a sip of the drink and gagged. I have never tasted a mixed drink; it was bitter. I couldn't let him think that I didn't know what I was doing. I took another gulp of the drink and forced it down. This time it was a little better. I looked his way again and smiled. I guess the smile was his sign to come on over which is what he did. I could have looked at him walk all night. He was dressed expertly in brown slacks with a smooth silk shirt and a brown rim hat perfectly tilted to one side.

"Good evening ladies my name is James. I couldn't help but notice you, fine ladies when you walked in the door. May I join you?" Cathy must have kicked my leg a dozen times under the table, I was sure I had a bruise the size of a grapefruit by now. Finally, when she realized that I couldn't speak she introduced the two of us. "Hello James it's nice to meet you, my name is Cathy and this is my friend Marie."

"Do you ladies come here often?" I know Cathy was waiting for me to jump in, but I couldn't think of a thing to say to him. "Well I have been here a few times, but Marie is new to the place. If you guys will excuse me, I am going to go to the ladies room for just a few minutes."

I wanted to strangle Cathy, why would she leave me at the table with this stranger? "Wait, Cathy, I'll come with you."

James grabbed my arm before I could get up from my seat. I sat back down in the seat and got lost in those big brown eyes. He leaned closer to whisper in my ear, "Would you care for another drink?" I could hear Mama's voice in my head, *Marie you know I taught you better than this.*

"Yes, James I would love another drink."

When Cathy returned to the table, James and I were on the dance floor. We danced the remainder of the evening. Finally, Cathy got my attention. We went back to the table. "It's getting late Marie we both have to get up early for work. We need to be getting back to the apartment."

I hated leaving James and the club, but I knew she was right. James came over and asked for my phone number. I kicked myself for not getting that cell phone when I thought about it.

I had to think about this for a moment. The only number I had was Mama's phone at the house. I wrote down my number at the store and told him when he called to leave a message, and I would get back to him. He didn't understand so I told him I would explain it to him at a later date. He wrote his cell number down on a piece of paper and handed it to me.

We turned and walked out the club. I could feel James watching my every move as we walked out the door. I was giddy with excitement all the way back to Cathy's apartment. Cathy let me sleep on her old lumpy sofa in the living room. It didn't matter sleeping was the last thing on my mind.

Cathy and I drove to the store together the next morning. We decided to meet for lunch. I was hoping that James would call the store today. He had given me his number, but I dared not call him first. I didn't want him to get the impression that I was desperate.

Time seemed to stand still. My mind was already imaging all the nights that I would spend getting to know James. I wanted to know everything there was to know about this wonderful intriguing man.

Life would be perfect if it turned out that *James was my CJ*.

God I hope you didn't break the mold after CJ. Thelma is not the only Rhoades daughter that deserves happiness.

8

The store was having a giant winter clearance sale. I barely had time to catch my breath, having lunch with Cathy was out of the question. In all the excitement, I forgot to check in with the call center operator to see if I had received any calls.

It was 5:45. I was scheduled to get off at 6:00 when my supervisor asked if I could work till 9:00. I wanted to say no, but I knew I needed the money, it wouldn't look good to turn her down. I was exhausted. I took a short 30-minute lunch. I was just about to tear into a sandwich when I remembered to check the desk for calls.

The call center phones were ringing off the hook with calls about the sale. When I walked into the room, she pointed to the employee boxes on the wall. My heart was beating so fast I could hardly breathe. I flipped through the messages. Cathy had left a message telling me she had to work late as well. Mama had called to see if I was coming home that evening and finally a message from James. He had called twice and left his number, asking me to give him a call.

I left the call office and went into the employee break room to use the pay phone. I had a reason to get a cell phone now. Mama thought they were a waste of money when you had a phone at home.

I prayed none of those noisy sales clerks were eating in the break room. I found some change in my pocket and dialed the number. I didn't need the paper I knew the number by heart. The phone rang once then twice; I was getting nervous and just about to hang up when he answered the phone, "Hello, hello." His deep sexy voice sent chills down my spine. "Hello, may I speak to James."

"Hey, Pretty Lady I was wondering if you got your messages."

"Yes, I got you messages the stores has been extremely busy today and I couldn't get away." My throat was drier than a dessert.

"What store do you work at Marie? What exactly do you do there?"

"I work at Wilson's Fine Clothing downtown. I am the lead sales clerk in the Women's Department."

"Oh, I see. Sounds like that keeps you busy. Well, Ms. Marie, what time are they letting you out of there tonight?"

"The store is having a big sale today and tomorrow, so I'm stuck here until 9:00 and I have to be back her tomorrow morning at 9:00.

"I would love to see you sometimes this weekend Marie. I mean if you are not too tired."

If he only knew how badly I wanted to see him, I could have run a marathon and still had extra energy for him. I had to keep reminding myself not to sound overly excited, "What are you doing Sunday afternoon, maybe we could meet someplace?"

"I don't know right this minute, but can I check with you tomorrow?"

"Sure that would be great. I have to get back to work, so I will talk to you tomorrow James."

"Okay Pretty Lady don't you work too hard, I can't wait to see you again. Marie is there another number I could call you? The store number is not going to work when you are away from the job."

My heart sank. There was no way I could give him Mama's phone number; she would have a stroke if a man called her house. I had to think of something, "James I have your number why don't I call you Sunday?"

"If you give me an *exact* time to expect your call I guess I can make that happen for you."

I didn't understand why I had to give him an exact time; I would be calling. I didn't want to lose this guy, so I told him to expect my call around 2:00 pm Sunday.

"Okay Marie 2:00 pm it is. That's when I will expect to hear from you right. Until then take care I will be thinking of you good-bye Pretty Lady."

The line was dead, but I was still holding the receiver waiting to hear his voice.

I went back to work in a daze. The remainder of the evening was spent trying to figure out how I would get Mama out of the house on Sunday so I could call James at 2:00.

I ended up staying until the store closed, and all the customers were gone. I was dead on my feet. I waited around for Cathy to give her a ride home.

I wanted to fall out on her lumpy sofa, but I knew Mama would probably put out an All-Points Bulletin on me if I didn't come home. It was after 11: 00 when I dropped Cathy off and started back for Claxton. I prayed all Mama's angel were awake and helped me drive home.

The Claxton River was wide awake as it moved swiftly toward its destination. The old metal bridge creaked and signed as I cruised across to the other side. The neighborhood was quiet and still. My block was dark; for once I hope Mama has gone to bed.

9

The glare from the headlights hit the front porch as I drove into the driveway. Just as I expected, Mama was sitting on the front porch with her Bible and all the angels in heaven.

I wasn't in the mood to argue with her. I prayed that I could just walk by and give her a kiss goodnight and go straight to bed. I was headed for the porch. Just as my hand grabbed the handle of the screen door, she started in on me.

"I guess I'm supposed to believe you have been working around the clock Marie."

I tried to ignore the sarcasm in her voice. Stay calm girl, "How are you this fine evening Mama? No to answer your question I didn't work around the clock. I worked late Thursday night. Then I spent the night at my friend's place because I was too tired to drive home. I got up this morning and went into to work at 8:00. I am exhausted. I am going to bed. I have to work tomorrow as well. I don't have the time or energy to argue with you, good night pleasant dreams."

"Well I suggest you take a shower before you get in my bed on my clean sheets; you smell like where you been."

I had no idea what she meant by that remark, and besides I really didn't want to know what she thought I had been doing. "Thank you, a shower does sound good. It will probably make me sleep even better."

It's just like Mama. She has to have the last word, "Marie you're moving too fast. You went and got this new job in town, and that car you didn't need and now you're staying out all night. All this is too much for a poor girl like you Marie." I had had about as much as I could stand. Why couldn't she just leave well enough alone for this one time?

"That car will be the ruin of you, Marie. You need to sell it, and then you can take a job back here in Claxton."

Hearing the word Claxton, made my blood boil. I should have just turned and walked away. But I couldn't allow her to win, "Mama the last time I looked at my driver's license the date indicated that I am twenty-two years old. I realize that I still live under your roof, but that does not give you the right to run my life. The way I see this Mama you had your chance at life, and this is where you ended up. But I want more and I believe I deserve more. I'm not doing anything to hurt you or anyone else. You didn't raise a fool, and I haven't forgotten what you taught me. So you are going to have to trust that I know what I am doing and have faith that you did a good job raising me. It's getting late Mama I'm going to bed, and I think you should as well."

I headed straight for the shower when I entered the house. I wanted to wash that entire conversation away. If only she could find something else to focus all of her attention on and leave me alone.

When I finished the shower, I walked into my bedroom and opened the curtains. The moon had followed me home, it lit up the night sky. I slipped under the covers. I wanted so badly to call James and talk to him before falling asleep, but I knew that was impossible with the mood Mama was in.

As I turned over in bed, I heard the front door close. Mama slid quietly past my bedroom. I prayed that she slept well. Within a few minutes sleep robbed me of my final thoughts. I tossed and turned most of the night after arguing with her.

I got up early the next morning to avoid having to say anything to her before going to work. I went into the kitchen and burned a piece of toast and drank a cup of lukewarm coffee before slipping out the door and into my car. Just as I turned the ignition, I looked up, she was in the doorway. I could tell she wanted to say something, but instead she turned and closed the door. She has never done that before.

I guess she felt that she had said enough the night before.

The drive to work was always pleasant. The roads are never busy on Saturday morning. I arrived at the store at 8:15. My shift didn't start until 9:00. I clocked in and sat down in the break room. I was about to get a cup of coffee when Cathy walked in. "Hey, Cathy I didn't know you were on to work this morning as well."

"Yea they put me down, and you know I hate working on Saturday morning; it cuts into my Friday night activities."

"Girl did you stay at home last night and rest up for our shift? I was dead on my feet when I dropped you off."

"You know I didn't stay home, on a Friday night are you crazy? I was dead tired as well, but I changed clothes and walked around the block to the joint on the corner. I hung out for about an hour and walked back home. I could have sworn that I saw a guy that looked just like that guy you met last night what was his name, John or James?"

"I'm sure it wasn't James; he didn't mention that he was going out last night when I spoke to him."

"Girl what's wrong with you, a man don't always tell you where he's going, did you forget that you just met this guy."

"Cathy, look at the time we will be late starting out shift if we don't hurry. If you need a ride home after work, wait for me in the break room. Don't work too hard."

I couldn't wait to get out of that break room and away from Cathy. She was my best friend, but I hated her no-it-all attitude. I understand that I didn't know James, but I think he would have told me if he were going out last night.

I headed toward my station. It was five minutes to nine. I had just enough time to call James. My body was on fire with the urge to call him. I looked around the store there weren't customers yet. I was back in the break room heading straight for the pay phone. I picked up the receiver and listened to the dial tone for about ten seconds before I dialed the number. The phone rang once then twice on the third ring I was just about to hang up when a voice, a female voice answered the phone. "Hello, hello who is this calling this number? Can I help you? State your business or hang up the phone,"

I was frozen in time, I didn't know whether to answer or hang up the phone. Who could this be? Why was she answering James' phone?

"Are you going to talk or what? I don't have time to play games?"

'I'm sorry ma'am I must have the wrong number, sorry to have bothered you." I quickly hung the phone back on the receiver and went back to work.

The store was a madhouse. Every woman in Mississippi must have come in, and tried on sizes sixteen to eighteen before asking for the size twenty-four that they knew they needed in the first place. I was dead on my feet when my shift ended at 6:00.

I finished with the last customer and ran to the break room. I knew my supervisor had to be looking for me to get me to close tonight. That was the last thing on my mind. I hurried into the break room and slipped into my coat. I thought about calling James one more time. He had been on my mind all day. I was frustrated and upset with myself the entire day. James had specifically asked me to call him on Sunday at 2:00. If I had just followed his request, I wouldn't have all these questions about the woman on the phone running through my mind.

I looked around for Cathy. I hoped she didn't need a ride. I had no intention of waiting around for her.

I walked out to the employee parking lot. I was about to open the door when Cathy tapped me on the shoulder, "Hey girl can I still get that ride?"

"Cathy you scared the daylights out of me. What are you doing out here? I didn't get off until 6:00."

"I hid in the break room from 5:15 to 5:30 so Stacy, wouldn't ask me to stay over."

"Girl I know you are so right about that. I prayed that she didn't come to the Women's Department. I wanted out of there. Get in and let's get out of here."

"I know you are tired Marie, but could we go to the club for just an hour before you go home?"

"Cathy I look awful. Don't you want to go home and freshen up a bit before going out?"

"No, I'm fresh enough right now. All I had to do was get out of that store, and my energy has returned."

"I don't know Cathy Mama is giving me a hard time about staying out, and I have to go to church tomorrow or she will have church service in the living room."

"We only have to stay for an hour; we'll leave when you say go. I'm just not ready to go to that lonely apartment just yet. Besides you know, you are dying to see if that new guy is in the club."

"I know James won't be there, he is expecting a call from me on Sunday. I told him that I couldn't see him this weekend. I'll drop you at the club Cathy, and I have to be getting back home. I don't have the energy to hear Mama this evening."

"No the club won't be any fun without you, so just drop me off at my place I'll probably take a nap and go out later."

After dropping Cathy off. I headed for home. I knew she was disappointed, but I wasn't in the mood for going out tonight. I just couldn't get the phone call out of my mind. I needed to know who the woman on the phone was and what was she to James?"

I turned the radio off in the car it was getting on my nerves. I drove back to Claxton with the hum of the engine and my thoughts. I didn't want James to know that I had called him when he specifically asked me to call him at 2:00-tomorrow afternoon. I guess I would just have to wait until the right time in the conversation with James and bring up the woman.

I let down my window and turned the radio back up. As tired as I was it wouldn't take much for me to fall asleep.

The Claxton River was nestled peacefully beneath the bridge as I continued my drive home. I couldn't imagine when Cathy could find the energy to go out again after last night. Maybe when I get home and get a nap I could give her a call. A little voice in the back of my mind told me; that's not about to happen.

10

Thelma was in the kitchen frying pork chops when I arrived home. She seemed genuinely happy to see me. Her schedule at the hospital kept her busy, so we hardly ever saw each other.

"Hey Marie, it's good to see you. I'll have dinner ready in a few minutes, why don't you sit down and talk to me for a while. We have a lot of catching up to do."

"Well, Thelma there is nothing new with me unless you call our mother driving me crazy something new. What's happening with you and the doctor?"

She turned around and sat down at the table with me. She reached for something in the pocket of the sweater she was wearing. She looked me right in the eyes and whispered, "You can't say, a word if I show you something?"

I could have strangled her it didn't take a rocket scientist to see she was holding a ring in her hand. I needed to see how big the rock was. I was dying to see the ring so I played along, "Thelma you know I can keep a secret, what's in your hand?" She opened the small black box, and I thought the sun had moved into the kitchen. I have never seen a diamond that big and shiny. I guess I must have lost my mind for a minute. I grabbed the ring from Thelma's hand and slid in on my right hand.

"Marie what are you doing? Give me that ring before Mama comes in and sees it?" "Thelma are you telling me that you are engaged, and you haven't told her?" How long have you had the ring and why on earth aren't you wearing it. Please tell me you said yes."

"I love CJ Marie, of course I said yes, but we have not told Mama. He wants to ask her for my hand. We got engaged last month on my birthday, but we have kept it a secret until he had time to get the ring sized. The ring belonged to his grandmother."

"So when do you plan on telling Mama, I hope it's soon. Maybe that will get her out of my business."

"CJ is going to church with us in the morning. Then he will come home for dinner, and that's when we plan on telling Mama."

"That sounds just wonderful Thelma. So you guys will be busy with her all afternoon at least until after 2:00."

"I would imagine, I know she will have lots of questions for CJ.

Marie would you please pray that Mama accepts my engagement. CJ makes me happy. Marie, Marie are you Okay?"

I guess I must have drifted off into a trance. I could not believe my Sunday afternoon was already arranged. I could not have asked for a better situation. Mama would be crazy by the time Thelma finished breaking the news about the engagement and she won't have any idea that I am on the phone with James. I wanted to twirl Thelma around in the room. Instead, I stood up and kissed her on the cheek and told her to check on her pork chops and stop worrying about Mama she would eventually get over it.

11

Mama was up with the chickens like she is every Sunday morning. She was at her best on Sundays. She would always tell us, "The Lord gives us six days to do our business and one day to take care of his business." It was always nice to hear her in the kitchen humming on Sunday morning. It's such a shame that it would all be over when Thelma breaks the news about the engagement.

I rushed out of bed and into the shower. When I finished dressing, I joined Mama in the kitchen with Thelma already seated at the table. She had prepared her usual feast for Sunday morning. She always made extra for the senior citizens who arrived at church early. We finished breakfast and dressed quickly to get to Sunday school on time.

We usually drove to the church together on Sunday, but I insisted that I drive my car this Sunday. I told Mama I wanted to get back to the house right after church so that I could take a nap; I said I was drained.

Mama and Thelma were about to pile into Mama's car when CJ drove up in the shiny blue Cadillac. The look on Mama's face would have stopped a train.

She turned to Thelma, "What is he doing here on a Sunday morning, can't you at least have one day away from him." All of the blood drained from Thelma's face. She looked as if she wanted to cry,

"Mama CJ is joining us for church this morning. We can all ride over in his car."

"That won't be necessary Thelma I am quite capable of driving myself to church, I have been doing it for over twenty years."

"As you wish Mama I will be riding with CJ. We will see you there shortly."

"Marie you are welcome to ride over with us."

"No, Thelma that won't be necessary I can drive myself to give you guys time alone."

Mama turned the corner on two wheels as she sped off in the direction of the church. The church was only about fifteen minutes from the house, and I'm sure she made it in five minutes.

I arrived at the church before Thelma and CJ. Mama was already fuming in the kitchen. Thelma and CJ came in a few minutes after I arrived. Sunday school was already in session. When Thelma walked into the sanctuary with CJ on her arm, you could have heard a pin drop. Every eye in the place followed her to her seat. It didn't take long for all the whispering to start. The remainder of Sunday school was a total waste of time. Not one person in the class had a clue about the lesson.

The rest of the service was long and boring as usual. Service was finally over around 1:00. I saw Mama chatting with a group of ladies. I was just about to make my exit when Thelma caught my arm and whispered, "The plan has changed Marie. CJ wants to speak with Mama after church. So the pastor will be present." I wanted to scream! She looked at me with pleading in her eyes, "Marie I know you are ready to go. Would you please hang around until CJ talks to Mama?"

I tried not to show the frustration I was feeling, "Okay Thelma I only have a few minutes."

Thelma grabbed Mama by the arms and asked her to come to the pastor's study for a few minutes. Mama was her usual stubborn self but with a little coaxing from the both of us she finally agreed.

We went back inside the church to the pastor's study. When we opened the door, CJ was in the chair by the window. Mama could smell a setup a mile away. She turned to leave the study, but I stopped her in her tracks. Pastor Carter walked over and led her to a comfortable chair next to his desk. "Sister Marjorie I'm so glad you could join us. Can I get you anything?"

"No Reverend I don't need a thing. I need to get out of this office and back to the kitchen to help the ladies serve dinner."

"I don't want you to worry about that right this minute Brother Morrison has something that he would like to discuss with you."

Mama was fit to be tied; she jumped up from her chair like she had been shot from a cannon. She was halfway to the door when CJ yelled, "Ms. Marjorie I want to marry your daughter!"

Thelma walked over and held Mama's hand with tears in her eyes, "Mama I said yes, please be happy for me."

Mama walked back over to the chair by the pastor's desk, she sat down and didn't say a word.

"Sister Marjorie are you all right? Can I get you a glass of water?" The pastor took Mama's hand trying to console her, "Sister Marjorie this is a nice young man, I think he will make Thelma a fine husband don't you agree Marie?"

Why the heck did he have to drag me into this drama, "Yes I think they will be very happy," I said half smiling.

The pastor rose from his seat, "Marie why don't we leave them alone for a while, we'll go and get something to eat." Mama was insane at this point. All she could do was sit silently on the sofa and pray.

I left the study with the pastor on my heels. We were headed toward the dining hall when I remembered I had to get home. I guided the pastor toward a group of older ladies and made my exit out the side door.

I was finally free of Thelma and Mama. It was only a few minutes past two when I jumped in the car. I hoped and prayed that James was still waiting for my call.

I think I broke the speed limit from the church to home. I pulled into the driveway. I don't remember entering the house, but somehow I must have because I had the phone in my hand as I dialed the number.

The phone rang once then twice, on the third ring that same female voice answered the phone.

I was determined to get to the bottom of this, "Hello may I speak with James."

"It's you again, the same one that called the other day, well sweetie James ain't here and if you know what's good for you, that's an answer to a prayer."

"Ma'am I don't know who you are, but James asked me to call him at this number at 2:00."

"You can tell time can't you, its 2:10. James waited for you about five minutes and he had to go and take care of his business."

"What do you mean his business...?"

"Listen, Little Girl you have no idea who you are trying to get involved with, take my advice and forget about James..."

"For your information I am not a little girl I am twenty-two years old and I can take care of myself...."

"Yea they all say that at first that is until James gets his hooks in them. Then they wish they had never laid eyes on James Littleton. Little girl James is not what you think."

Another female voice came ringing out from the distance, "Liz I'm hungry is James back yet with the food?"

My head was spinning I didn't know what to do, "Ma'am what the heck is going on here, and who is that in the background calling for James?"

"Little Girl like I told you, you don't know James. The girl you heard in the back ground and me are just two of James' associates, now I got to go, James will be back any minutes. You listen to me; I don't need you running your mouth off to James. Do yourself a favor and stay away from him."

Bam! I jerked the phone away from my ear as she slammed the receiver down.

I walked into my bedroom and fell on my bed. I closed my eyes and replayed the conversation over and over in my head. I didn't know who to believe. I knew I had to do something I had to know if Liz was telling the truth.

I got up. The phone was still in my hand. I dialed Cathy.

It was time we made another visit to the club.

Cathy answered on the first ring. I told her I wanted to go back to the club. She was probably half dressed before I hung the phone up. I told her I wanted just to check the club out for about an hour. Since it was a Sunday evening, I figured there wouldn't be too much action. Besides I knew I needed to get back home to check on Mama. After the way I left her in church, she would be ready for the asylum by the time I returned home. I changed clothes. My new pink pantsuit would be perfect. I didn't want to look sexy; I wanted James to know I meant business. I put my hair back into a ponytail. I did my best thinking with my hair up. I wanted to prove to Ms. Liz that I wasn't like the girls that James usually picked up in the club.

By the time, I arrived at Cathy's house it was almost 4:00. I blew the horn. I needed her to hurry up. I wanted to be back home and in bed by 7:00.

Cathy finally emerged from her apartment with her new black skirt and patent leather pumps. When she sat down in the car, I thought, she had fallen into a field of roses. She must have bathed in the new fragrance of the month from the store.

We arrived at the club a little after 4:00. Just as I imagined, it was pretty dead. Cathy could have cared less she couldn't wait to get on the dance floor. I took a table in the corner not too far from the door, so I could see everyone coming and going. The waitress came over, and I ordered a glass of soda. I didn't want anything stronger because I knew I would have to drive back home alone. Cathy finally came back to the table. I asked her to watch my drink so I could go to the ladies room. I went to the ladies room and took care of my business avoiding the stares from all the lonely desperate women. I didn't feel like talking to a bunch of man hungry woman on the prowl for new meat.

When I opened the door to the ladies room and looked toward my table, it was evident that Cathy was gone, but I certainly didn't expect to see James in her place. I couldn't have been in the ladies room more than five minutes. It's hard to believe Cathy couldn't even wait that long. My hands were shaking. I was so nervous. I walked back to the table. James looked up at me and smiled as I sat down. I didn't know what to say, I had so many questions that needed answers. "Good evening, James. How are you?"

"Hello, Pretty Lady I certainly didn't expect to see you here this evening."

"No, I decided to get out after church since it didn't look like you and I were going to talk. But I did get to speak to Liz, and she explained the situation to me." The smile and the twinkle in his eyes disappeared at the same time.

"Well, if you recall I believe I told you to call me at 2:00. I had other things to do, and I couldn't afford to wait around for your call. What exactly did Liz tell you about me?"

"Well, Liz is not one of your biggest fans. She said I would be wise to stay away from you. She said you were bad news, and I would get hurt."

"Well Pretty Lady, Liz has a big mouth and if she is not careful someday someone is going to close it for her. But for now I guess I have to ask if you believe everything she told you?"

"I don't know what to think James. I did just meet you, and you have all kinds of mysterious women living with you, and you haven't told me who this Liz woman is?"

"Liz is none of your business she is a part of my past. That's as much as you need to know. Now, why don't you drink your soda and we can go outside for some air and talk this thing out."

"No, I'm not thirsty anymore I just want to be getting home. I think I'll just get Cathy and get out of here."

"I believe that we have a lot more to talk about, so why don't you drink your soda and give me a chance to explain, it's not all that late."

"I'm sorry James, I should be going if I could just find Cathy. Maybe you can explain some other time."

"No! I'm going to explain now! Now sit down and drink your soda before all the ice melts. I don't want to cause a scene, but you need to do as I say!" His eyes were cold and dark as night. I didn't want anything to do with this man that was sitting across the table from me. I was frightened. I picked up the glass of soda from the table and took a sip, it didn't taste anything like soda. James put something in my drink that's why he was so desperate to get me to drink it. Oh God, what was I going to do? I can't do this. It's no telling what James has planned for me. I scanned the room hoping that Cathy was close to the door, so when I made my exit, she would be right behind me. Cathy was nowhere in sight. I hated to leave her, but that was my plan as soon as I figured a way out of this mess.

James looked at me without batting an eye. "I know what you are thinking and it won't work. There is no way you are getting out of here without drinking that soda, so you may as well go ahead and get it over with."

"James I don't even know you. Why are you doing this to me?"

"Well, Little Girl you are just like all the rest of the stupid woman that come in this club. Coming in here picking up men is a game to you. Well, I'm going to play the game with you. Now drink up, we have some place to go." He moved the glass closer to me.

With my left hand, I reached for my purse. I made sure it was securely in my hand. Then I picked up the glass of soda. The waitress was headed my way. She was carrying a tray of drinks. I knew this would be my only chance to escape. She was just about to pass the table when I threw the soda at James. I pushed the waitress down as I got up from the table and ran toward the front door.

I was in my car in a flash. As I sped out of the parking lot, James exited the club. He ran in the direction of my car screaming and yelling profanities at the top of his lungs. From my rear view mirror, I could see him pulling out his phone. I figured he was calling his next victim. One thing for certain I wanted nothing more to do with James Littleton.

James

Alright, Ms. Marie, you are going to pay for the little show you put on tonight! You can bet on that. By the time, I get through with you. You will be begging for mercy. I got your number I just need to put a few things in place, and pretty soon you will be mine. For now you drive home and pretend that you have seen the last of me.

What the hell is wrong with these women? They come out to the club to meet a man, and when a real man shows up, they start with all these games. That's okay cause they learn real fast that I am in control. I am not a man that you can mess with.

Damn, my head is killing me. I hate it when I get upset like this. I left my pills in the car. I needed to go back in the club to make sure I haven't missed any fresh meat. Forget it, ain't no need in going back in the club, half of them in there belong to me anyhow. I got to get home and take care of this mess with Liz and her big mouth. Then I need to call my folks on the inside and tell them I have another fish on the line.

My head is out of control, this pain is too much. I can't believe I let these whores upset me like this. Where is my medicine?"

12

MARJORIE LINDA RHOADES

Reverend Carter followed me as I ran from his office. "Sister Marjorie I don't think you are in any condition to drive. Why don't you sit down and settle yourself before you leave? Everything is going to be alright. It's time to let the girls go; you have done an excellent job raising them. Now it's time for them to find their way in life?"

"Reverend I know you mean well, but you don't know the whole story. I just need to get away and be alone for a while. I will be fine don't worry about me." I have never been one to say anything negative to the Man of God, but the reverend didn't know how close he was coming to getting a fist right in the middle of his head. I had to get out of there. The nerve of the pastor. He was going on and on about Brother Morrison being such a good man. What did he know about Brother Morrison? That was probably the first time Brother Morrison has ever set foot in a church. How did he know that he was a good man? Lord have mercy how could Thelma have agreed to marry this man without even talking to me about it. I guess she has her mind made up. Thinks she's in love. What the heck does she know about love? All men ever do is use you up and then leave you high and dry with a bunch of kids that they don't want.

Lord, what am I going to do? I certainly can't go home now. Marie will probably be there. I'm liable to give her a piece of my mind. I know she helped Thelma plan this whole thing. I may as well go to the grocery store and pick up a few things. That will relax me a bit. That's one place I don't have to worry about seeing either of my daughters. Hopefully, Marie will be long gone when I get back home. The silence in the car was deafening as I drove through town. I couldn't stand the sound of anything other than my own thoughts. I had to park at the rear of the parking lot, which is unusual for a Sunday.

Why is this store so darn crowded on a Sunday afternoon? I guess everyone is getting ready for Memorial Day holiday. My God you would think Save- A- Lot was having a giveaway on pork ribs.

Grocery shopping is not any fun with the store being this crowded. I'll grab a few things for the week and get the heck out of here.

I raced up and down the aisles fighting baskets and out of control children along the way. The checkout lines were longer than usual and the store never put anything, but these sinful magazines up front. I hate seeing these things. Is there nothing else going on in this store?

I glanced to the right. I noticed a women seated in a wheelchair. She was slumped over and leaning forward. She was coming toward me. She looked like she was about to meet the mayor. Why on earth would anyone have on a hat with a veil and long sleeves in this stifling heat? Why is she so covered up? God help me I hated to stare, but I couldn't help myself. I had to move closer to get a better look. Something so old and familiar drew me closer. I jumped across to the next checkout lane, so I would be directly behind the well to do figure in the chair. The ladies' attendant pushed her forward when I moved behind the chair. She leaned over and whispered in the veiled ear of her employer. Then she turned quickly to go back into the store to gather the items she had forgotten. As the attendant walked away, the veiled figure gracefully raised her arm to dismiss her. I had to grab the magazine rack to keep my composure. There it was on the middle finger of her left hand, *the ring, my ring*. The ring that everyone one living in Lady Bee's house wore at all times. The ring that signified that we belonged to the house and Lady Bee. This veiled figure in the wheelchair had on my ring.

I couldn't take my eyes off the darn thing. As the woman gently rested her arm on the handle of the wheelchair the sleeve of her blouse moved slightly to reveal deep, puckered scars on her hand and arm. Her burns were quite severe. The injuries took my breath away. My head began to spin. *There was fire blazing all around me. I had to get everyone out of the house. Why did Lester have to be such an old food and bother me? I had to get out of the house. I yelled and screamed as loud as I could. Oh God, please make sure everyone get out safely!*

"Lady are you alright? Do you need me to get you some help?" I turned around as a red-haired, freckled face kid was urging me to get out of his way.

"I'm alright son. Why don't you go on ahead of me?"

Get a grip on yourself Margie, You're just tired. It can't be her this couldn't be happening. How had she survived the fire? Could this be her? I simply had to know. I waited until the attendant returned and completed her transaction. I completely forgot about my items in the basket. Nothing seemed as important at the time. As they were leaving the store, the attendant pushed her companion down the sidewalk to Russell's Pharmacy. She rolled the wheelchair to a space in the corner. She went to check on the prescriptions. I rushed over to the bench in the corner to sit down.

The late afternoon heat was beginning to take its toll on the veiled figure, causing her to drift in and out of a restless sleep. I got up from the bench. I had to go over to the wheelchair; now was my chance to get a closer look at the ring. I had to be sure.

My heart was racing. My palms were sweating. Large drops of sweat were taking control of my face. One glance at the ring caused my heart to skip several beats. It was the replica of the one I had thrown out so many years ago.

The ring covered most of her finger. There were arches on top and the bottom. The turquoise leaves and beads were in a perfect circular pattern with a large blue tiger eye stone in the center. My past was staring me in the face. I knew this was a sign from God. The demons that I had locked away so many years ago were wrestling to be free. I had to come to term with my sins.

My focus returned as the booming voice of the pharmacist called her name, "Francis Antoinette Delacroix your prescriptions are ready." My questions had all been answered it was Francis Ann; my closest friend at Lady Bee's house. I was the reason she was in that chair. I turned to take one last look then I walked out of the pharmacy in a daze. She didn't say a word maybe she didn't recognize me. I got into my car. I sat there unable to move. My mind was racing, as tears ran down my face. Francis Ann, my protector. She had survived the fire. Had she been living in Claxton all this time, so close and I didn't even know?

God give me the strength to go back and make things right.

The knock on the window startled me back to consciousness. It was the same freckled face kid, "Ma'am are you Okay? Do you need me to get you some water? You're soaking in sweat."

"Thank you, son. I'm fine. I forgot to roll down my windows." I flashed a smile at the kid and started the car. I knew what I had to do. After seeing the shape, Francis Ann was in and knowing it was my fault. I had no intention of dealing with any foolishness from Marie. I knew Thelma would be out with her new fiancée, doing God knows what. I didn't have time to think about that now. I had to go back to Memphis. It was time to fix everything that I buried so many years ago. My car apparently knows it way home. When I drove up Marie's car was not in the yard. Thank God the house was empty and quiet. Marie must be out trying to figure out how she is going to get herself out of her mess. She's just like her daddy. God knows that man put his brand on her. You can't tell her anything. She has her life all figured out. I know she has herself involved in some trouble. If she thinks for one minute, I don't know she's out in the club all night and getting involved in who knows what. If only I could tell her my real story.

There have been so many times I wanted to sit the both of them down and tell them why I can't leave Claxton? Claxton is the only place I've ever felt safe. It's the only place I've ever felt like I belonged. Lord, are you punishing me because I kept my past hidden from my girls? Maybe this is payback. The scripture says you reap what you sow. I have sewn my share of bad seeds. I never claimed to be no saint, but Lord I asked forgiveness for everything I did in the past.

I don't know how I can ever forgive myself for what I did to Lady Bee and poor Francis Anne. It's been twenty years since I left Memphis. I should have gone to try and fix what I did to her. How could she ever forgive me for everything I took from her? The memories of that awful night make their way into my thoughts every day. If only there were some way I could make it right.

I have to get out of here. Maybe Mrs. Larson is not too busy on a Sunday evening. I've always been able to talk to her about everything. I need to tell somebody the truth, even if it's just to hear myself say the words.

The girls don't understand my relationship with Mrs. Larson, but that old lady has been there for me more times than I care to remember. She's been the best friend I could have every asked for over the past few years. Mrs. Lena is really like a mother to me.

When Arthur left with that other woman, I nearly lost my mind.

With two small children and no money. She was truly a God send.

I turned the car around and drove toward her house. My mind went back to memories of the fire, and Francis Anne. How could I ever face Lady Bee after seeing Francis?

My God why didn't I say something to her, Francis looked so frail. Her burns had to be pretty severe for her to be veiled. She used to talk about her kids all the times; I wonder are they taking care of her? God! Where are you? I need you to tell me what to do?

Oh my God! It was almost 6:00 pm. I can't bother Ms. Lena with this problem. Sunday is her only day with Mr. Larson. I'll talk to her in the morning. I'm exhausted.

The sun was setting and the night breeze felt wonderful as it drifted through my window. When I got home, the house was still dark. The girls hadn't made it back.

I stumbled into the house and went straight to my bedroom. I closed my door and turned out the lights. I wanted nothing to do with Thelma or Marie.

13

Marie

My head was pounding I drove like a bat out of hell to get home. How could I have been so stupid and immature? Cathy tried to tell me I didn't know what I was getting myself into. But no I had to go and get myself mixed up with James the Crazy.

Mama's car was in the driveway. That was a good sign at least she didn't go off the deep in and drive over the bridge. Now if I could just get in the house and into bed without a confrontation that would be a blessing. Thelma was still out with the good doctor, which was a smart move. I eased into the house, her door was closed, It's clear she wants nothing to do with us. I ran to my room and closed the door. My bed was calling to me, and I couldn't wait to answer.

I drifted in and out of sleep most of the night. Every time I closed my eyes I saw James' cold black eyes staring down in my face. How could I have been so stupid to have allowed myself to get caught up in this situation?

As I lay in bed, I wished I was thousands of miles away from this place, and even further away from this life. I finally drifted off to a restless sleep.

I could have thrown the clock out the window when the alarm went off at 6:00 am. I lay in bed wrestling with the idea of calling in sick. I have a perfect attendance record. If nothing else I was always faithful old Marie. I heard Mama stirring in her bedroom and decided that staying home was a horrible idea. I had no intention of listening to her complain about Thelma and the good doctor all day long.

It didn't take long for me to get in the shower. Mama was in the kitchen when I finished dressing

I silently prayed, Lord, please shut Mama up this morning. I'm not in the mood. I just want to get in and get my morning ritual; coffee and burnt toast

"Good morning, Marie."

"Good morning Mama, can I get you a cup of coffee before I leave for work?"

I knew she was ready for a fight. She was fully dressed, hair rollers, robe, and house shoes were long gone.

"I'm sure you knew Thelma was going to pull that stunt on me yesterday. You don't even need to deny it because I don't want you lying this early in the morning. Besides Ms. Marie you probably thought it was funny."

"Well, Mama since you have everything all figured out, there's no need to discuss this matter any further; you have a wonderful day." I grabbed the cup of coffee spilling it all over the floor. "Sorry about the mess, I guess I'm in a rush. I'm in no mood to get into anything with you today."

"So now I have to clean up your messes too. You and your sister will learn one day that I know what I'm talking about…."

"Goodbye, Mama." I was out the door before she had a chance to utter another word.

14

Marjorie

Thelma stayed out after midnight on a Sunday. She did it on purpose, so she wouldn't have to face me. If she only knew I didn't want to talk to her anymore that she wanted to speak to me.

The Reverend was right, my girls don't need me. They probably won't even know I'm gone. I'll take off a few days and let them fend for themselves. I have to go and take care of this business. I'll leave them a note so they won't worry, or at least I pray they would worry where their mother has gone.

It was after nine when I got to Ms. Lena's; I was only a few minutes late. She will probably give me her speech about tardiness that I have heard a thousand times.

The driveway was empty I guess Mr. Larson has already left for the office. I never understood why a man in his 70's would get up every weekday morning and go into work when he turned the business over to his son years ago, or at least that's what he called it.

Ms. Lena was seated in the kitchen when I arrived. She looked over at the coffee pot when I stepped into the kitchen. I guess that was my signal to get her some coffee. "Good Morning Ms. Lena how are you feeling this morning? You look mighty pretty with your hair down. Did you sleep well?"

"Good morning Marjorie, you're a little late this morning. Is everything Okay?" I continued to make the coffee along with her breakfast. Now was the perfect time to talk to her about my situation.

"Well, Ms. Lena I would like to discuss a situation with you if you feel up to it."

"Why don't you finish my breakfast first then you can sit down and tell me all about it. Are you having trouble with your daughters? It wouldn't surprise me one bit if that Marie was in some trouble.

"No ma'am Ms. Lena it's not my daughters this time; it's me. My past has been chasing me for years, and I'm just tired of running."

I placed the plate of food in front of her and poured myself a cup of coffee. I hardly knew where to begin.

Sensing my hesitation Ms. Lena got up from the table and poured herself another cup of coffee. "You know Margie the best place to start a journey is always at the beginning that way you just follow the path that's already in front of you."

I didn't want to cry. But at the time crying was easier than talking. When at last I found my voice I began to tell my story.

"Ms. Lena I haven't always lived in Claxton. I was born here, but I ran away when I was almost sixteen. I ended up in Memphis. I did a lot of things to survive. I lived with other runaways in a house run by a woman named Lady Bee. There was always something going on in that house. Half the time I didn't know whether to be happy or scared out of my mind. I lived in the house for almost four years. I couldn't take it any longer. I didn't want that life anymore. I tried telling Lady Bee, but she just wouldn't listen."

Ms. Lena continued to eat her breakfast as if she didn't hear a word I said. At last she looked up from her plate, "Marjorie truth is the only way to take the sting from your past. You should know by now that nothing you could say would ever change the way I feel about you. Would you mind getting me another cup of coffee?"

Tears ran down my face as I filled her cup. I sat down in the chair and poured my heart out to Ms. Lena. When I finished the story, I felt the weight of the world lifted from my shoulders. When the words ceased to flow, I got up from the table and cleared the dishes. Ms. Lena continued to sit at the table as if I had just exchanged my favorite meatloaf recipe with her.

"Well Marjorie I don't know what I am going to do without you for a few days, but I guess me and that old man will have to make do. You go home and pack a bag and get back here as soon as you can. You need to get on the road to Memphis before it gets too dark."

"Ms. Lena I didn't say I was going to Memphis right away. I just needed to talk to someone. I've never told another living soul about my past."

"Okay, you told me. Do you feel better? Your friend has been waiting twenty years to hear you say the same thing. You go ahead and get a bag packed and get back by here as quick as you can. Marjorie, I know you want to share this with the girls, but you can do that when you get back. Don't allow your mind to talk you out of doing what you know you have to do. Marjorie, I know it will be hard, but it's best not to leave any messages telling the girls where you are. They will assume that you are working for me. Don't worry if Marie comes looking for you I will make up something. Hurry go get your things and get back here I have something for you.

I stood there in the kitchen speechless. In all the years that I have worked for the Larsen's, I have never hugged either one of them. I didn't know how she would react and at that moment it didn't matter. I hugged the frail seventy-year-old frame and whispered, "Thank you I won't be gone long."

As I took the short drive back to the house to pack my bag, I feared that Thelma may not have left the house. Was I relieved when I saw my prayers were answered? The house was just as I left it.

I went out on the back porch to get my old suitcase; it hadn't been used since I got back from Baton Rouge. That seemed like so many years ago. I pulled the bag in from the porch. I packed enough clothes for an overnight visit. I didn't want to stay any longer than I had too. I know Ms. Lena warned me about leaving a note, but it just didn't feel right if I didn't say something to the girls. I wrote the first note and left it on the counter by the coffee pot. I went back and picked it up and put it in my pocket. I tore another sheet of paper from the pad scribbled a note:

Thelma and Marie,

A lot has happened over the past few days. I need time to get my head on straight. I will be staying with the Larson's. I need the time to get the house ready for the upcoming holiday season.

I hope and pray that you girls know that I love you more than anything. Everything I have ever said and done was only to make your lives better. Take care of yourselves. Please don't worry about me. Marie, please don't worry Mrs. Larson.

Mama

I rushed back to the Larson's home. Ms. Lena was dressed and waiting for me. I thought for sure she would have asked me to prepare lunch for she and Mr. Larson, but instead she took my hand and placed a white envelope in it. She told me to take my time and take care of my past. I took the envelope and left with tears in my eyes.

I knew it would be hard to fight the demons of my past, but I couldn't go on living with this guilt.

15

MARIE

I think I drove on two wheels all the way to work. I wanted to be anywhere that wasn't near Mama.

Cathy was already in the break room when I arrived. She was the last person in the world I wanted to see.

"Hey girl before you start yelling at me, would you please just give me a chance to explain."

"Cathy I don't want to hear any of your excuses; you left me in the club…"

"Girl, that James is crazy. He made it clear that if I liked being healthy it would be best if I left. Marie I did try to argue, but James is kind of persuasive if you know what I mean. I told him that you were my best friend, and I just couldn't leave you stranded since I was the one that introduced you to the club in the first place. Before I knew what was happening, he grabbed my arm and pushed me out the door."

"Cathy I am so sorry that you had to go through that, he didn't hurt you did he?"

"No, he didn't hurt me, but one thing for sure he scared the life out of me. I don't want anything else to do with that brother."

"I didn't know he attacked you. I freaked out when I got back to the table, and you weren't there. James was sitting there smiling looking like the devil himself. His whole attitude had changed. He made it clear that I wasn't leaving the club without him. I was terrified. He ordered me a drink and insisted that I sit and drink with him. I knew something had to be wrong with the drink. He was practically forcing it down my throat. When I refused to drink it, he started threatening me. "Marie please tell me that you didn't."

"Girl you must be crazy I am way ahead of you on that one. I kept him talking because I knew what he was planning on doing. I waited until the waitress came by with a tray of drinks. I took my drink and threw it in his face. I pushed the waitress down and ran out of the club."

"Well, Marie I guess this means you, and I have to find us a new club."

"I guess you are right because I have no intention of ever stepping foot back in that place again."

"Well, I'm glad we both got out alright. Look at the time I have to get on the floor. Let's try to get together for lunch if the floor is not too hectic."

"OK, Cathy we'll see, I'll talk to you later."

I waited until Cathy left so I could have my cup of coffee in peace before I headed for the floor. With coffee in hand, I headed for the table when I noticed something in my box. I didn't recognize the handwriting on the envelope, but I was hoping and praying it wasn't Stacy asking me to stay till closing tonight. I sat down and opened the envelope. My heart skipped a beat, my hands shook uncontrollably, and the room started spinning all around me.

Hey, Pretty Lady. I hope you didn't think you had seen the last of me. Now that really wouldn't be any fun would it, especially since you and I didn't part on the best of terms, and we do have some unfinished business to attend too.

You see Pretty Lady I plan on us having a very long and profitable relationship. I would highly advise you to listen if you plan on staying healthy. I'm running this show, and you'll be doing everything I say. I'll give you all the details of our little arrangement when you call me at exactly noon. Don't be late, I hate to be kept waiting.

I think you know who,

My hands were shaking like a leaf on a tree. What did James want with me? What did he mean by arrangement?

It was after 8:45 I was still in the break room. I couldn't move. I knew I needed to get up, Stacy would be blowing a fuse if I didn't get to work, but none of that mattered to me at that moment. My life was about to change. Nothing good could come from an *arrangement* with a fool. Mama's voice was ringing in my ears, "You and your sister will learn someday that I know what I am talking about."

I hated it when that old lady was right; which is most of the time.

I didn't know if I was selling clothes or horses. My mind was spinning in circles. All I could think about was calling James at 12:00 noon. I had no idea what he could want with me. But I knew whatever it was it wasn't good.

The store was a mad house. The customers were in and out of the dressings rooms all morning. I prayed that no one was shoplifting. The way my mind was turning they could have probably stolen the entire store, and I would not have known the difference.

Finally, when I couldn't handle the suspense any longer, I logged out of my register. It was 11:50. I went straight to the break room and prayed the pay phone was available.

Just my luck, the break room was packed. Both of the pay phones were being used. What time is it? Oh my God its 11:55. Spinning on my heels, I turned around I remembered there was another phone in the reception area. I didn't want to have a conversation with James out in the open, but I didn't have a choice.

The security guard was seated at the desk when I arrived. "Hi, Frank how are you doing today?"

"I'm fine Ms. Marie how are you?"

"Well, Frank I would be doing a lot better if I could use the phone for just a few minutes. Both phones in the break room are being used, and I have an urgent matter that I need to attend too."

"I understand Ms. Marie, but you know I could get in a world of trouble if I let you use this phone."

"I wouldn't ask if it weren't an emergency Frank, and I promise I won't bother you again. If you can just give me five minutes of privacy, I will owe you big time."

"You want me to leave my station. Girl you are truly trying to get me fired!"

"I don't want that to happen, Frank; I just need you to take a five minute restroom break, or go and take a smoke break. Believe me I wouldn't ask if I didn't need too."

"Okay, Ms. Marie I do need to go to the restroom. If anybody walks up to the desk have them to sign in, and I will be right back. When I get back I need you already off the phone; I hope you understand?"

"Yes sir I understand, and I appreciate your kindness."

It was 12:05 when I finally dialed James' number. I couldn't believe that I was calling him back. The phone rang four or five times before someone finally answered.

"Hello."

Oh my, God, it was Liz again. I didn't want to get into a confrontation with her, "Hello Liz is James in he asked me to call him."

"Yea he told me you were going to call him at twelve on the dot unless you can't tell the time it's after 12:00 which means you are late. Believe me that is going to cost you, Little Girl and you can take that to the bank. You had no business blabbing your big mouth to James about what I told you. I got your number. I don't give a damn what James does to you from now on."

"I told you my name was Marie and I am not a little girl. Don't you talk to me like that ever again Liz. I am not afraid of you or James. Now is James available or not?"

"Shut UP! I'm tired of talking to you. No! James left at 12:00. When you didn't call, he told me to tell you that he would give you one more chance to get this right and call him at 5:00."

"What do you mean it's going to cost me?"

"I tried to warn you to stay away from James, but you just like all the rest. You never listen. If you were smart, you would pack a bag and get out of town and never come back to Franklin again. James is not the type of man to mess around with."

"Like I told you Liz I am not afraid of James. I can't imagine what he wants from me. I hardly even know him."

"Before you get out of this mess you will wish you had never met James. James is a user Little Girl, and you got something that he can use." "I don't have anything that James can use, you must be crazy."

"You are one dumb Little Girl, you are like all the rest. You work in a clothing store don't you?"

"Yes, but."

"Then you will be supplying James with the clothing for his women and men. I've said enough if you got any sense in that head of your, you would leave town today, but if you plan on staying I wouldn't miss calling James at 5:00."

"Like I said I am not afraid of James. I am not leaving town."

"Suit yourself Little Girl, by the way, my favorite color is blue."

The phone went dead in my hand. I stood motionless staring at the wall.

"Did you make your call Ms. Marie because I need to get back to my desk? Ms. Marie are you Okay? You look like you drank a cup of poison."

I didn't notice that Frank was back at his desk. He took the receiver from my hand and placed it back on the headset. I walked back to the break room.

The remainder of the day was a blur. I was scheduled to get off at 6:00. At 4:30 I couldn't take it any longer. I told Stacy that I wasn't feeling well, and I needed to go home. She didn't like the idea, but she wanted me to come back tomorrow, so she told me to go home and get some rest.

I don't know or care how I got down to the corner store. I needed to use the pay phone. I had no intention of missing the five o'clock call with James. I needed this time to give him a piece of my mind and get this business over with once and for all.

The corner store was overcrowded as usual. I walked in and went straight to the back for a cold soda. It was a hot, humid day. My throat was dry as a dessert. The soda felt good going down. I fidgeted in my purse for the number then realized I didn't need it. The number was a part of my brain.

The phone rang once, twice, three times everything in me said hang up and take Liz's advice. James finally answered on the fifth ring.

"Hello, Pretty Lady I was expecting your call. I'm going to forgive you for not following my earlier instructions; it's going to cost you."

"James I don't know what kind of sick game you think I am going to play with you but."

"I need you to shut up and listen if you want to keep that mother of yours nice and healthy."

"What did you say? Did you just threaten my mother?"

"Yes, I did Pretty Lady I said your mother and that newly engaged sister her name was, oh yea Thelma. I guess I have your attention now. You see Pretty Lady we are business partners, you just became my newest supplier. I call the shots, and you will do as I say. Now find a piece of paper to write this information down. Follow my instructions to the T do you understand? Are you still there?"

"Yes, I'm still here."

"When you get to work tomorrow, I want you to go to the women's shoes. I need three pairs of the new black heel pumps that just came; they have the alligator look on the front. I need a size 8, 9 and a 9 ½. Then go into the women's ware section. They're a new black and gold pantsuit that the store just got in. I need it in sizes 8,

10, and 12. I will give you until Saturday to get all this together. Don't even think about telling the police or anyone else for that matter. I will know.

When you have everything call this number, and I will tell you where to bring the stuff. Well, Pretty Lady don't disappoint me. I will hear from you on Saturday."

"James how am I supposed to pay for all these items? I love my job, and I have no intention of stealing merchandise."

"Pretty Lady that's your problem, you can steal the stuff, pay for it, or stand on you head. That's not my problem, but the one thing you had better not do is miss my delivery on Saturday. I guarantee you won't like me when I get angry. And, by the way, don't take off early any more people may start to get suspicious." The phone went dead as I stood there listening to the dial tone for what seemed like an eternity.

All of the air must have left the room. I couldn't breathe, I could hardly see. The room was spinning. What was I doing in this situation? I looked up to heaven.

God, I haven't been bad all my life. I know I can be stubborn at times, but I don't deserve to go out like this. And even if I don't deserve your help, Mama and Thelma certainly do. I know you already have angels at her side. Please, God, I need your help.

I guess I didn't realize how loudly I was praying. All of the men in the store had taken their hats off. As I walked out the door, all I could hear was Amen. I smiled, paid for my drink, waved goodbye, and hung my head in shame as I walked to my car.

There was no joy in the drive across the bridge back to Claxton. The radio was a nuisance. The sight of the birds flying overhead was getting on my nerves. I had to figure out a way to get out of this mess. I've never stolen a thing in my entire life, and I had no intention of starting now.

I was overjoyed when I walked in the house and Mama, and Thelma were nowhere in sight. I walked into the kitchen and put on a pot of water for coffee. When I opened the cabinet to get the coffee. There it was in the back of the cabinet. Mama's rainy day stash. She kept it in a coffee can. The can called to me like a wolf howling in the woods. I could just take a couple of hundred dollars bills. That would take care of this problem. Mama never counts the money she just adds to it when Mrs. Larson pays her on Thursdays. I don't know why she just won't put the money in the bank like normal people. I guess she doesn't trust other people handling her money. The can was suddenly in my hand. I sat down at the table.

There had to be over a thousand dollars here. Surely she wouldn't miss a couple of hundreds. I sat there for a minute my imagination was going wild, Satan was getting the fire and brimstones ten times hotter for me. I couldn't steal from my mother. I put the money back in the can. Stealing is not the way to get out of this problem. Marie, what is wrong with you? I know there has to be another way out of this mess. My coffee was still where I left it. There was a note on the refrigerator. It was Mama's handwriting, probably her grocery list for the week. I didn't have the energy to deal with anything. My bedroom was calling me. I needed the quiet to help me think.

It was almost 6:00 Cathy would be getting off soon, I had to tell someone what James was doing to me. I put my shoes back on and headed for the front door. CJ and Thelma were pulling into the driveway. I tried to rush to the car, but Thelma was so excited she was glowing.

"Hey Marie, how was your day?"

"It was Okay. I'm really in kind of a hurry I can't talk to you about it now."

"Well, Marie I need you to pencil me into your busy schedule. I'll need my sister to help me plan my wedding. She extended her hand to show the diamond ring she was finally wearing. We set a date for November fifth teen. We have a thousand and one things to do. Marie are you listening I said we set a wedding date."

"That's nice Thelma I am so happy for you and CJ. I will carve out some time for you next week I promise, but right now I have to go."

I got into my car and pulled out of the driveway as tears ran down my face and made puddles in my lap. Thelma's smile filled my mind. My sister was the happiest she has ever been.

The look of joy on her face was priceless. I hoped at that minute CJ would make sure she was always smiling.

I couldn't believe I was mixed up with a fool like James.

I prayed that Cathy had some idea how to of get me out of this mess.

I pulled out of the driveway and headed toward the bridge. The river looked so peaceful and calm. If only that were true.

My thoughts were spinning in my head. Suddenly, it hit me like a ton of bricks. I slammed on the brakes as if a bolt of lightning had hit me. I looked around. I was in the middle of the bridge, thank God there was no one behind me. What is the matter with me? I've known all the time the good doctor was my way out. It was time to put my plan into action. I made a U-turn in the middle of the bridge and headed back home.

I was out of the car and on the porch before the car was in park. I almost had a heart attack when I looked through the curtain. Thelma and CJ were sitting in the living room. But, that couldn't me my sister making out with a man. That was a sight that I wouldn't soon forget. I made a noise on the porch before things got heated up.

When I walked in Thelma jumped up and straightened out her skirt. CJ sat up and smiled with Thelma's lipstick all over his face.

"Hey guys hate to interrupt, but I forgot something in my room."

"That's Okay Marie we were just talking."

When I got to my room I sat down on the bed. I had to get CJ to come in here away from Thelma. He was going to give me a loan to get out of this mess.

"Thelma would you mind if CJ helped me get a box off the top shelf of my closet?"

CJ yelled back, "Of course not Marie, I'll be right there."

He walked into my room. My goodness, he was gorgeous. I hated to let him leave. Thelma was one lucky lady. Gorgeous and rich too. I waited until he was inside the closet before I approached him.

"CJ I am so sorry to bother you, but I need your assistance, but I can't talk to you about it here, can I come by the hospital tomorrow afternoon?"

"Marie are you in trouble, maybe we should tell Thelma what's going on I wouldn't want anything to happen to you and she not be aware of the situation."

Oh God, they were made for each other, they were both worry warts. "No, I don't need you to tell Thelma, it's not that big of a deal. Can I come to the hospital and talk to you or not?"

"Of course you can Marie. I have rounds until 11:00, but I should have a few minutes after that. I am working on the 5th floor tomorrow just ask someone when you arrive. The nurses will show you where I am."

"Thanks, CJ I'll see you tomorrow."

"Marie what do I tell Thelma I was moving in your room."

"I don't know be creative. You'll think of something."

I made small talk with the love birds until I couldn't stand another minute of the two of them. I had to get out of here. It was time I drove back to the store and see if I could catch Cathy.

16

I was still smiling at my good fortune when I arrived at the store. I waited for Cathy in my usual parking space. She should be coming out of the employee exit at any minute. I couldn't wait to tell her what this fool is trying to me make me do.

I was getting worried. It was after 6:00. Her new manager was about as bad as mine, about asking her to stay over and work.

After a few minutes, Cathy came out of another door. She was looking around the parking lot as if she was expecting someone. I was just about to blow the horn when a white Chevy pulled in and headed for a spot at the rear of the parking lot. Cathy started walking in the direction of the car. Maybe she didn't see my car. I've never seen this car before, but she obviously knew them. She opened the back door and slid right in.

There were two men in the car. They sat in the car for a few minutes then Cathy got out and leaned over in the window to talk to the driver. She pointed to a large dumpster by the back gate. She reached into her purse and gave the driver a slip of paper. The driver gave her an envelope with something in it, and she turned and walked back to the store.

I didn't know what was going on. I sat there trying to figure out why Cathy would get in the car with these strange men? Maybe they were just strange to me; from the looks of things Cathy knew them quite well. I waited until she had walked back into the store.

I sat in the parking lot for what seemed like an eternity. I started the car and was about to drive off when Cathy came out the employees exit. She spotted my car and started walking toward me. What was I supposed to do, just pretend I didn't just see the whole episode with the men in the car?

"Hey girl what you are doing back at the store, I heard you got sick and had to go home."

"Yea I was really tired, so I drove around for a while.

I didn't feel like going home and dealing with Mama and Thelma, so I thought I would come by the store and give you a ride home. Are you just getting off?"

"Yea I had to work late to put out the new shipment of shoes that just arrived. I'm starving would you like to grab a burger or something?"

I didn't know whether to scream at her for lying to me or tell her to get the heck out of my car. It's really none of my business. It shouldn't bother me what Cathy does. She can associate with whom she pleases. She has her secrets, and I certainly have mine.

"A burger sounds great let's go to the new place over on State Street."

"That's fine but would you mind driving me to the apartment first I have to change these shoes my feet are killing me. Can you believe it I sell shoes for a living, and my feet are on fire."

We engaged in small talk on the drive to the apartment. "It will just take a minute to change my shoes."

Cathy jumped out of the car and left her purse on the floor. I was dying to see what was in the envelope the man in the car had given her. The curiosity was killing me. I leaned over and picked up the purse. The envelope was right on top. I know my heart skipped a beat. When I opened the envelope, a big wad of cash was staring me in the face. Oh, my God! It took every ounce of restraint in me to put that money back in her purse. Being tempted twice in one day was bit much. I could probably give Satan a match at this point. I glanced out the window as Cathy was coming down the steps. Just as I was about to put the purse back, it slipped from my hand and fell on the floor.

"That was quick. Girl, I'm sorry about your purse I was trying to borrow your lipstick when your purse slipped from my hands."

"No, problem."

She reached into her purse and gave me the lipstick.

"Why don't you just keep it?"

We drove over to the burger joint. I don't think I heard a word Cathy said at dinner. All I could think about was that large wad of money in her purse, and how all my problems would disappear if I had just a couple hundred.

I continued to pick at my burger until I couldn't stand it any longer.

"Cathy I'm really tired I'm going to get home and try to get some sleep."

"You do look like you are kind of out it, I don't think you heard a word I said tonight. Marie is there something bothering you that you need to talk about? Is there anything I can help you with?"

"I'm just a little tired Cathy, and I need to get home, I have to be at the store at 8:00 in the morning.

Cathy if you were having a problem with something you would tell me, you know you can trust me right?"

"I got the ticket girl it was my treat; you're right it's getting late we better get going."

She skated right past that question like a professional skater. Cathy is in pretty deep if she can't even tell me what going on with her.

We drove back to her apartment in silence. There wasn't much to say. The secrets between us filled the car.

"Good night Cathy see you at work tomorrow."

"Good night Marie, be careful driving home. I hope you feel better."

17

There was no joy in driving home across the bridge. All I wanted to do was get to bed and sleep for days. I realized I'm not cut out for this sneaking around and keeping secrets.

It was after 10:00 when I got home. Mama's car is usually standing guard in the front yard at this hour. Something was going on with Mama it's not like her to be out this late on a weeknight. Maybe she had to work late for that old witch, Mrs. Larsen. I hope that's all it is. When I'm rich, the first thing I'm going to do is get her out of that old women's house.

The lights were on. Thelma was home. The good doctor was nowhere in sight. I hope he didn't blab his big mouth and tell Thelma I'm meeting him at the hospital tomorrow.

After easing the front door open. I slipped into my bedroom, quietly undressed and got under the covers. I was in no mood for conversation with Thelma; sometimes she is as bad as Mama.

I wanted so badly to fall asleep and awaken and realize this mess was all a dream. The day's activities had taken a toll on me. I was out like a light.

I heard movement in the kitchen around 7:00 the next morning. I didn't want to believe it was morning already. I could have stayed in bed all day. I had a feeling I was going to be late this morning.

Thelma had coffee ready for me as I dashed through the kitchen. There was still no sign of Mama. If she was trying to get us to worry about her, she was doing a great job. "Thelma have you spoken to Mama; she wasn't here last night when I got home." "I found this note from her on the counter." Thelma had a look of concern on her face.

"What does the note say? She must have been upset with the both of us if she left a note."

It says that she needed to clear her head, and she will be staying over at old lady Larson for a couple of days. She is trying to get a jump on the holiday cleaning."

"Have you talked to her? I mean it couldn't be anything else. You know how upset she was about your news."

"No, Marie I haven't spoken to her since yesterday. I know she was pretty upset about the new, but I'm sure the idea is settling in by now. Don't worry she will probably be home by Thursday."

That was my clue to make my exit. I certainly did not want to entertain another conversation about her and CJ, "Well girl you are probably right, I am going to be late so I better run I'll talk to you later. By the way, Thelma are you scheduled to work today?"

"Yes, but I go in at one I'm covering a shift for a friend of mind. She needed to be off this evening. I'll probably get stuck pulling an all-nighter."

"Oh, that's very thoughtful of you. What floor are you covering for her?"

"She usually works in maternity so I'll be helping with deliveries all evening."

"Okay, well you have a great day, and I'll see you tonight; if you're lucky. If you get a chance, I guess one of us should call and check in with Mama to make sure that old hag, Mrs. Larsen hasn't killed her."

"Yea you're probably right I'll give her a call on my break today."

Everything was set and in place. I'll go into work and take my lunch break at noon; then zip over to the hospital to hit up the good doctor for the cash and get back to work. I'll have one of the other sales clerks cover for me if I am just a few minutes late.

I clocked in after 8:00. I knew Stacy had probably put out an APB on me. The sales floor still had boxes of merchandise that needed to be unpacked when I got to the floor. It's not like they don't work us to death as it is without requiring us to help the night crew with stocking merchandise.

The new line of summer stock was beautiful. I couldn't wait to pick out my new outfits as I usually do. I heard James' voice ring in my ear Pretty Lady you better have my order ready. Reality hit me in the face like a bull in a China shop. I wouldn't be getting a new outfit this week. I hated James for what he was making me do. As I looked over the new stock, I recalled the list of items James had given me.

How did he know there was new merchandise coming into the store at this particular time? Why did he even need this stuff? What kind of game was he playing? I felt sick.

James had someone watching me. I hated the thought of someone knowing my every move. I would never feel safe in this store again. My body went numb. How did he know about Mama and Thelma being engaged? I didn't like him knowing about me. A voice in the back of my head was telling me to wake up and quit playing dumb. I looked over the clothing in my hand; I was certain that one of the outfits had to be for Liz. If that cow thinks I'm getting her an outfit in blue she is sadly mistaken. I continued to peruse through the merchandise until I had the sizes he had requested.

The only person in this store that knew everything about my life was Cathy. Maybe it wasn't a coincidence that she left me at the table the night James acted a fool with me. Why all of a sudden did Cathy have a purse full of money and new friends with a white car? Oh my God how could I have been so stupid I hardly knew Cathy, and she knows everything about me?

Panic set in. I had to get a handle on myself. I would have to be careful about everything I said to Cathy. Right now I needed to hide the three outfits that I needed for later. Then I would have to get those shoes from Cathy's department without answering a thousand questions. She was already on the floor when I walked over. She wasn't getting a word out of me, she could think whatever she wanted about James from now on. My lips were sealed.

"Good morning girl, how you feeling? Maybe you should have taken the day off and rested up before you came back. You know how this store gets when there is a sale."

"I'll be fine. Have you put out any new shoes?"

"I'm in the process of unpacking the boxes. I should have them unpacked and out before the store opens. Was there anything in particular you wanted to see?"

I wanted to scream and tear all her of hair out. She was trying to pretend like she didn't already know what was going on. It's not like James hadn't already filled her in. She had probably picked out the sizes and had them ready in the back. "Yes, I'm looking for the new black pumps that you just got in."

"You need more than one pair; I can set them aside for you until you get off."

"Why would you assume that I needed more than one pair?"

"I didn't mean anything by it, Marie, I just thought that maybe you were looking for a pair for you and your sister. I know she would like the pump."

"Well I do need three pairs can you just show me where they are in the stock room and I will put them aside."

"Marie are you Okay; you look really tired and stressed? You know you can tell me if something was wrong."

"What could be wrong? You already know everything that's going on in my life. I just have a lot on my mind. Please show me where the shoes are I have to get back to the floor."

"Give me the sizes you need Marie and I'll put them aside so you can get back to work."

"Are you sure that won't be a problem for you I wouldn't want you to go out of your way for me."

"Marie I don't know what is going on with you, but you have to believe that I am here for you, and you can trust me."

"Cathy I would love to believe that, but I just don't know, so much is going on and I ...."

Stacy came up behind me as if out of thin air. "Marie I need you get back to you station, there are still quite a few boxes to unpack before the store opens."

"I'll get everything out and on the floor before the store opens Stacey I always do. I'll talk to you later Cathy."

I walked back to my department with thousands of questions floating in my head. Something was not quite right, but I couldn't put my finger on it.

The customers piled into the store like ants at a picnic. I didn't want to be bothered with all these women who have not accepted reality and continued to try on dresses that God in heaven knew they would never in a lifetime be able to wear.

Finally, it was 11:30. I didn't take my morning break, and I wouldn't be taking my afternoon break, which would give me ninety minutes to get to the hospital and back by 1:00.

18

I skirted out the back door and over to my car. It didn't take long to get over to the hospital. I parked in the emergency room parking lot and prayed that the guard was not making his rounds.

CJ said he would be on the fifth floor. Thelma was in the maternity ward. There was no chance of running into her. The elevator to the fifth floor was crowded.

The nurse's station was busy with nurses and other staff members going and coming.

"Excuse me, nurse." I stood there wondering what you had to do to get someone attention? "Excuse me, nurse."

Forget this I'll find CJ's office on my own. The other end of the hall was empty. Not one single nurse turned to ask where I was going. I guess since I looked healthy no one cared.

At the end of the hall, there was another hallway leading to a corridor where the doctor's office were. I went through the double doors and kept walking. At least I was away from the patients and the nurses. At the end of the hall on the right, there was a sign on the door, Dr. Morrison Chief of Surgery. It wouldn't hurt to check in on dear old dad, maybe he could tell me where his handsome son was.

The door was slightly ajar, so I didn't bother to knock. His office was spacious and furnished nicely. Thelma is one lucky woman. Imagine being a part of all of this. There were voices coming from the other room. I recognized the doctor's voice, but not the female voice.

I'll just have to check this out. I do need to get dear old dad's attention. The guy had only met me one time, I hope he remembered me.

Oh, my God! Have I hit the mother lode? The sight of the good doctor with another woman in his arms on the couch made my heart skip a beat. I would never forget the look on his face.

He was so busy with his lady friend he didn't even notice I was in the room. I stood there for a few minutes just enjoying the view. Who would have thought the good doctor was cheating on his wife, and the nerve of him to get a white woman?

There was no way the good doctor would allow his secret to get out. It sure as heck would cost him to keep me quiet. I turned around and politely took my seat in one of the comfortable leather chairs in his office. I had no intention of leaving even if it meant I would be late getting back to work.

After about fifth teen minutes, the room was silent. I guess the lovebirds were finished. I walked over to the door of the other room. It shouldn't take that long to do I had to do. I had to go back to work as sometime. I peeped into the room again, the white woman was still lying in his arms. She looked so quiet and peaceful, he looked like he had won a million dollars.

It made no difference to me who he slept with, as long as he paid me to keep my mouth shut.

It must be true what they say, you can feel it when someone is staring at you. The good doctor looked toward the door and almost needed surgery on his own heart when he caught a glimpse of me standing there. He waved a slight gesture for me to move away. I resumed my position in the leather chair.

It didn't take the doctor long to throw his clothes on and get his butt out here in his office. The look on his face said it all; I had him just where I wanted him.

"Hello, Mary or it is Marie I know you are Thelma's sister. We only spoke that one time at dinner."

"I'm just fine Dr. Morrison as a matter of fact my life just got a whole lot better."

"I guess you are wondering what I am doing with another woman in my office, well let me explain…."

"That really won't be necessary Dr. Morrison, save your explanation for your wife."

"Marie I assure you that won't be necessary, you see Marie my wife is not a well woman and I really would hate to burden her with undo stress. After all, we are about to be a family in a few months."

"You know you're right and families do take care of one another. So I am going to need you to help me as I help you by keeping my mouth shut about the way you spend your lunch breaks."

"How can I help you, Marie?"

"Well for starters I'm thinking of a figure in my head, can we say three hundred a week for starters."

"Marie I'm not the type of person that you want to try and blackmail. Can we be reasonable? I can give you say a thousand dollars now, and we can call it even. I'm sure you've never in your life had that much money at one time. I do know where you came from."

"I guess you are right Dr. Morrison that is a lot of money for a poor girl raised on the other side of the river. But you see Dr. Morrison I was raised on the wrong side of the river, but I never accepted that life as the only life I would ever have. My mother did the best she could, and I am grateful. But that's just it, that life was all my mother could give me. I have always known that I deserved better, and you are going to help me get it. When I decide this arrangement is over, I will leave town, and you will never have to see or hear from me again. Your secret will be safe with me. As I said, we can start with three hundred dollars a week. I'll need the first payment today, and the payments will be due the same time each week. Do we have an understanding, doctor?"

"You know Marie you are nothing like your sister Thelma, I guess my son did get the better one of the two of you. I guess that will be cash? Marie, I am counting on your discretion.

"You know it doesn't matter what you think of me Dr. Morrison, I see people like you every day in the store. They come in thinking they are better than me because I work an honest job for a living. Even you probably think because that white woman is sleeping with you that somehow makes you better than the rest of us. I dare you to ask yourself would she give you the time of day if your name weren't on that door."

The good doctor strolled toward me with the money in his hand and fire in his eyes. If it were at all possible, he would have strangled me and thrown me out the window. I knew then that this wouldn't be a long-term arrangement. As soon as I figured out a way to be rid of James and save enough money to get out of Claxton, Dr. Morrison would be history.

"Here is your money Marie. By the way, you don't have to drive to the hospital every week, we can make arrangements to meet some-place else."

"That's fine with me. I'm sure you don't want your lady friend to think you are trying to replace her.

I rose from my seat and headed for the door. It's a pleasure doing business with you, I'll see you next week Dr. Morrison."

I should feel bad about for what I was doing to CJ's dad, but the truth of the matter was I didn't. As far as I was concerned he deserved to get caught. His poor wife probably worked her finger to the bones putting his sorry behind through med school, and this is the thanks she gets. Come to think of it three hundred is too low, I'll wait a couple of weeks and then ask for five hundred a week.

I surveyed the corridor trying to locate a clock. I hated hospitals with their military time. I knew I was going to be late getting back to work. I would tell Stacey I was visiting a friend at the hospital and lost track of time. At this point I didn't care, in a few months I would be out of the Claxton.

The elevator was coming down when I pushed the button. The door opened, CJ bolted toward me with the biggest grin on his face.

"Hi, Marie I'm sorry I got caught up with an emergency sorry I missed our meeting. Why don't you walk with me to my dad's office so we can talk?"

"CJ that won't be necessary I have to be getting back to work. Besides I worked the problem out. Why don't you give your dad a few minutes? Give him a little time before you go in there. I think he may be a tied up with something."

"Why would you say that Marie have you seen my dad?"

"I passed by. He looked like he was in a meeting give him a few minutes. You have a great day CJ."

"Marie I'm having dinner with Thelma later, would you like to join us maybe we can talk then. I hate keeping things from her."

Where is the darn elevator? This guy can't take a hint. "No, I have plans, enjoy your dinner."

The security guard was headed toward my car when I made it back to the parking lot. "Hello, officer you have a nice day I am getting my car out of your way."

I raced back to the job with the money in my purse. I hated having all this cash, and I couldn't spend a dime on myself.

Cathy was waiting in the break room for me when I got back to work. She was getting on my nerves with this best friend act she was giving me.

"Girl where have you been, I thought I was going to have to perform CPR on Stacey I knew any minute she would blow a fuse."

"Don't worry about me Cathy, I will take care of Stacey. I had some business that needed to be handled. I plan on working through my afternoon break to make up the time."

"Is everything alright you look a little stressed?"

"I'll be just fine Cathy when I get back to work, besides you have enough to worry. I mean with all the extra things you have going on."

"What are you talking about Marie, what extra things?"

"I don't have time to get into it now Cathy, I just thought you and I were becoming good friends, at least enough to trust each other when we had a problem."

"What do you mean Marie? I have asked you over and over did you need to tell me something. I knew something was going on with you, but you wouldn't open up to me about it. And now you come in here giving me this lip about you can't trust me."

"Whatever Cathy I don't need you to confide in, I don't need anyone."

I stormed out of the room and back to the sales floor. I had scarcely put my purse away when Stacey came breathing down my neck.

"I have been looking for you; I have other employees that are ready to have lunch. Where have you been?"

"I had to visit a sick friend at the hospital, and I simply lost track of time, it won't happen again. I will work through my afternoon break to make up the time. If you will excuse me, I have to take care of these customers."

The remainder of the afternoon, my mind was going in fifty different directions. I just couldn't believe that my life had become so complicated.

I'm taking all the merchandise to James at one time. I put the outfits in an area of the women's wear that didn't get much traffic. I'll take the clothes today and get the shoes on Friday. I didn't want anyone to get suspicious and ask about my new found wealth. The thought of giving all this new merchandise to James, which I could have for myself made me sick. I wanted to ram my fist right down his throat. That was not possible as long as James was threatening my family. James was a user, and he would get what's coming to him in due time. I was pretty sure I was not James' only victim. Guys like him always have other innocent, unsuspecting women taking care of him just like me.

When my shift was over, I picked up my stash of clothing and went to the register. I opened my purse and saw the folded bills. That money felt so good in my hand. I wanted to caress and hold it forever. My heart melted in my chest. For the first time in my life, I had money that I didn't have to work hard to get. There was so much good that I could have done with this cash. Mama's voice interrupted the thoughts in my head, "You got that money the wrong way, Marie. It serves you right that you won't get to keep it." Mama was right I was doing the same thing to Dr. Morrison that James was doing to me. I guess I was no better than he was. It was no use dwelling on that now. I was up to my ears in this mess.

Cathy came over as I was finished checking out my items.

"You have quite a few outfits girl. Aren't you a size 10 Marie? Why would you need those other sizes? I know you are not buying them for

Thelma?"

"You know Cathy you just do not get the hint. I would appreciate if you stayed out of my business. I can buy clothes in any size I want."

"I realize that Ms. Marie, but you are buying clothes, and it is not even payday."

"Cathy have you cleared your register today? I think the shoe manager is waiting for you." Stacey seemed to appear out of nowhere again.

"Marie it looks like you got some nice things. You sure you got all the sizes you needed?"

Both of these sistahs was getting on my nerves, "I'll see you in the morning, Stacey."

"You know I have you down to open in the morning Marie."

"No, I did not know that. I usually close on Wednesdays."

"I know, but I thought you could use a change."

"Whatever I'm tired. I got to get out of here."

Anger and frustration were getting the better of me. Not knowing what was going to happen next was not easy for me to digest. I hated the thought of going home and dealing with Mama and Thelma, but I was too tired to find someplace else to hang out.

I drove down by the river. I got out of the car for a minute and watched the lights dance on the water. Sometimes I feel as though this river was my only friend. Tears rushed to my eyes. I didn't want to cry. Crying wouldn't help my situation. I have never felt so alone in my entire life. Even in the worst of times I could always count on Mama and Thelma being there when I needed them. I don't know what I would do if James hurt either of them. The river couldn't solve this problem. It was time to go home and face the music.

Mama's car was still nowhere in sight. This thing with old lady Larson was getting out of hand. The note said she would be staying a couple of days, but I didn't see why that would be necessary. I had a good mind to drive over to old lady Larsen's house and drag Mama back home. I needed her to be home tonight. Besides she hates sleeping away from home. I know the thought of sleeping in the guest house is driving her crazy. She's probably missing me and Thelma; she could probably use the company. I hate to admit it; I miss her nagging.

The car was in reverse. I drove through town to the grocery store. I picked up her favorite donuts before I headed over to Mrs. Larsen. Everything in me said park in the front driveway, get out and walk right up to the door and knock. But I knew Mama would end up paying for my antics. I drove around to the back alley near the guest house. Mama's car was nowhere in sight. It was after 7:00. Mama would not be caught in a chariot from heaven at this hour. I hope that old witch did not send her to the store this late. I just had to know where my mother was. That meant that I had to knock on the front door and give the old lady a heart attack.

I pulled the car around to the front door and parked on the street. I knew all the neighbors were probably dialing 911 by now. I rang the doorbell and waited. I could see someone coming down the stairs through the curtains.

"Yes, who is it?" A dry old voice rang through the front door.

"Mrs. Larson, its Marie, Ms. Marjorie's youngest daughter. I am looking for my mother. I was wondering where she might be?"

"Wait just one-minute dear, are you alone?"

"Yes, ma'am I am. Do you need to see my driver's license?"

"That will not be necessary, dear I am aware that Marjorie has two daughters."

The front door opened, and she motioned for me to come into the foyer. "You are the youngest daughter, the one that is always causing Marjorie to worry."

"As I said Mrs. Larsen I am looking for my mother." She mentioned that she would be staying over here for a few day."

"Your mother is not here. She will be out of town for a few days. She told you girls that she was here so you would not worry. But it appears her business is taking her longer that she thought."

"Well, Mrs. Larsen since you seem to know where she is and what she is doing, could you possibly give me a number to reach her. My sister and I are pretty worried about her."

"There is no need to worry, your mother is perfectly fine. When she finishes her business, she will be back. When I speak to her, I will tell her that you came by to see her. It is getting late dear, and I must be getting back to bed."

I was so angry at that old witch I wanted to drag her old wrinkled body up the stairs just to throw her down again. The nerve of her not telling me where my mother was. The veins in my neck were on fire, and my fists were clenched. I closed my eyes and took a deep breath. When I opened my eyes, I saw a vision of Mama at the top of the stairs. I took that as my sign from God to get the heck out of there. I turned and walked to the door. I just had to say something to this old woman, "Regardless of what you might think of me, I do love my mother. Would you please tell her that when you talk to her."

I just had to do something. I opened the door and slammed it behind me. I prayed that I had broken something very expensive.

I stood there on the porch as anger filled every fiber of my body. Old lady Larsen is one lucky lady. If she only knew how close she was to rolling down those stairs, she would not have talked to me the way she had tonight.

I'm tired of playing games with her. Tomorrow If I don't hear from Mama I'm going to march back over to the plantation and demand to know where my mother is. But for now, I have got to get to bed. I can't believe Stacy put me on to open in the morning after working late today.

The house was silence when I go home. Thelma said she would probably have to work over tonight. I guess that means I'm on my own. I couldn't remember when was the last time I had taken the time to eat. I stumbled into the kitchen. I took out the leftovers from Sunday's dinner. It was just like Mama to have enough food for an army. She still cooks enough to feed the neighborhood. I had a wonderful midnight snack in front of me. Mama had prepared all of my favorites, but I didn't have the appetite for Mama's chicken without her presence. I put the food back in the fridge. I walked to Mama's room and opened the door. I prayed that old woman was alright.

It was so peaceful in Mama's room. It hasn't changed since we were kids. There is always a place for everything, and everything is in its place.

Her collection of dolls was still standing guard on the chest in the corner.

I took one long look at the room. I didn't want to forget one detail. It felt as though all of this would be taken from me one day.

I turned and closed her door and walked back to my bedroom. The moon said goodnight as it hid behind the clouds.

Mama where ever you are, please take care of yourself your baby girl needs you.

19

Thelma

I have been stuck at this darn hospital all night long. I can't wait to get out of here. "Hey, Thelma how is everything going in maternity today?" I don't know why Lisa is trying to speak to me. It's not like I don't know she can't stand me.

"Girl it has been a zoo and I can't wait till I get out of here. The first thing I am going to do is soak in a hot tub of water."

"What time do you get off?"

"I should have my notes wrapped up in about an hour." It's not like she isn't one of the reasons I had to work over last night.

I couldn't wait to get away from her, man is she, one nosy nurse. She would give anything if she knew I was having dinner with the most handsome doctor in the hospital. We would be making funeral arrangements if she knew he belonged to me. I liked the sound of engaged. I wished my mother felt the same way.

Mama should be home by now. I didn't want to let Marie know that I was worried about her as well. Marie doesn't understand that Mama has to work for Mrs. Larson. That's the only job she could get. Besides the lady is more like a friend than her employee. I'll give her a few more days then I'll check with Mrs. Larson myself.

I wonder where my handsome fiancée is taking me to dinner this evening. It doesn't matter as long as I am with him.

My notes are done. I am out of here before they ask me to stay another shift. It would be just my luck that someone didn't show up, and they ask me to stay this morning.

Okay, got my purse and my keys. Dang it! There's Kelly; her mouth is already fixed to say Thelma can you stay over. Well, the answer is no!

"Thelma, how are you this morning. Are you leaving so soon?"

"Yes, Kelly I am dead on my feet. I am getting out of here."

"Well, I was going to ask you to help us out for a couple of hours until things slow down. Then I remembered you had already worked a shift for a friend, I guess you do need to go home sometimes, even if there is no one to go home to."

"I guess you are right Kelly I'll just go home and curl up with a warm glass of milk and a hot bath. See you tomorrow."

I can't wait to send her the first wedding invitation. No better yet I'm going to hand-deliver the invitation to the nursing staff, so I can watch the expressions on their faces. The best part of all will be handing in my letter of resignation, then announce that I will be working in my husband's new office uptown. Just a few more months. I can hardly wait.

I smiled all the way to the bus stop. I love taking the bus home. I know Marie thinks I should get myself a car, but that would mean fewer opportunities to ride with my fiancée. Besides I get to talk to my old friends if I ride the bus home.

The bus was crowded as usual at this time of morning. Everybody was rushing to get work.

My stop was coming up next, "Goodbye, Ben, have a good day. Did you get that medication my doctor friend prescribed for you?"

"Oh yes, ma'am tell him thanks again that the cream is clearing that problem right up. I can't wait till he gets his new office open. The wife and I will be his first patients."

"Oh, you're too sweet. I'll make sure I tell him, have a good day."

The walk from the bus stop was a little less than a block. The way my feet were hurting it felt like a mile. From the distance, I could tell neither Mama's car nor Marie's was anywhere in sight.

I wonder how Mama would feel if Marie or I did the same thing to her that she is doing to us. Treating us this way, is so unfair. Mama acts as if we don't care about her. If she would just let go and allow us to live our lives.

I still expected to greet Mama in the kitchen; even though I knew she wasn't home. The house was so quiet without her. I hope she knows that her daughters are missing her. *Lord just let her be alright.*

Okay Thelma that's enough of that. Mama is fine. What time is it? It's a little after nine. That gives me enough time to straighten up the house a bit; I know Marie doesn't have to be this messy. CJ gets off around 11:00. He should be here shortly after.

I finished the dishes and washed a load of laundry. My feet were still on fire, so I guess it's time I soaked in a warm bath.

I went straight to the bathroom and turned on the hot water. I poured in half the bottle of that new bath soap Marie gave me for my birthday. It would be just perfect this evening.

The minute my foot hit the water, all the tension of the night was gone. I could have stayed in the tub all morning. Sleep rested on me like a new blanket.

Knock, Knock. "What is that? Oh my, God, I fell asleep in the tub. That must be CJ, and I'm not ready. "Wait a minute I'll be right there! CJ is that you?"

"Yes, Thelma are you expecting any other doctors?"

"I'll be right there, give me a minute!" I'll just throw my robe on and let him sit in the living room while I get dressed.

What am I going to go with my hair the ends are all wet? I must look a mess. I stopped dead in my tracks when I saw him standing on the porch. God, the sight of that man takes my breath away. He brought me flowers again. God whatever I did to deserve this, thank you a thousand times over.

"CJ I look a mess give me a minute to get dressed, and I will be right with you."

"Aren't you going give your fiancée a kiss, you look good to me all the time."

"Stop it I look horrible. I fell asleep in the tub. I guess I was tired, and it hit me when I relaxed in the tub."

"You don't have to apologize. What is that fragrance you are wearing? You smell like heaven."

"It's a gift from Marie."

"Remind me to thank her and tell her to do it again. Now come here so I can kiss my lovely fiancée."

"I couldn't resist him. I didn't want to resist him. I melted in his arms. I was totally at ease. I never wanted him to let me go. CJ covered me with kisses. His mouth was everywhere. I never wanted this to end. His hands felt like butter as he touched every area of my body. I couldn't help myself. He looked me in the eyes I knew he wanted this as badly as I did. I heard the promise I had made to Mama ringing in my ears. I promised her I would wait. Why wasn't that promise enough at this moment? All I wanted to do was show this man how much I loved him.

I took him by the hand and led him to my bedroom where he closed the door, and the walk to heaven began.

When I woke up, I was still in CJ strong arms. I eased from his embrace and dressed quickly. I hated to wake him while he looked so peaceful and content, but I couldn't take the chance Marie or God forbid Mama walking in the door.

"CJ, CJ sweetheart you have to wake up. We have to get dressed."

"Thelma I haven't rested like this way in years. Come here lay down beside me."

"No sweetheart we have to get up before someone comes home and finds you in my bedroom. I don't plan on answering a thousand questions."

"I love you Thelma Rhoades and you don't have to answer to anyone. If anyone has a problem with what just happened then they need to talk to me. You belong to me, Thelma. I mean that I belong to you for the rest of my life."

I leaned over and kissed the love of my life. "Well, sir if I belong to you, it's time you feed me. I'm hungry after that workout."

"Speaking of workout, am I going to have to wait until we are married to get another workout?"

"Hold your horses' big guy you have to feed me first and then we'll talk about additional workout sessions. I think we can work out some arrangement. I wouldn't want us getting out of shape."

We finished dressing just as Marie's car pulled into the driveway. I could tell she was in a foul mood, she slammed that car door as if it were her worst enemy. Whatever her issue was, it was not going to ruin my evening with CJ. We crossed paths on the front porch.

"Thelma have you heard anything from Mama. I went over to that that old witch's house last night. She had the nerve to tell me that she knows where Mama is, but she was not going to tell me. Can you believe that, the nerve of her not telling me where my mother is? I tell you if Mama is not home by Saturday I am going to drag the truth out of her."

"Marie I'm sure Mama would appreciate all this caring and affection that you are showing when she gets home. No, I haven't heard a word from Mama. But as you said Mrs. Larson knows where she is. At least we know she is Okay. She has had a lot to digest Marie she probably just needed some time to get away. She will be back when she can deal with the situation. Don't stress yourself out and for God sake, please don't go back and say anything to Mrs. Larson. Mama would hate it if you upset her."

"I guess. But this is so unlike her to disappear like this. I don't know how to take her behavior. I'm sorry my manners are horrible this evening, how are you CJ?"

"I'm fine Marie if your sister would feed me. Would you like to join us for dinner Marie?"

"No that's sweet of you to ask, but I know my sister cherishes every minute with you and I don't want to intrude. I'll find something in here to snack on, and probably get in the bed."

"Marie you wouldn't be intruding. Why don't you join us for dinner? You can take your car so when you finish you can leave, and CJ and I can finish our evening."

"Thanks, guys. I didn't feel like being alone this evening. I promise I will eat and get out of your way. CJ lead the way I am right behind you."

20

Marjorie's Journey

I drove by the old house on Murray before I left town. I wished life could be as simple as it was back then. I sat there a few minutes just thinking and reminiscing before I decided it was time to go.

Claxton had long since disappeared from my rear view mirror, but I could not stop myself from occasionally glancing in the rear view mirror just to make sure. After a few hours of driving the only reminder of Claxton was the river as it snaked a path in the distance. I imagined the river had a great laugh at me for thinking I could get away this easily. The road ahead continued to twist and turn like the thoughts running through my head.

I had no idea what I hoped to accomplish by leaving town. I knew every bone in my body said go. I have not felt this kind yearning and turning to leave in over twenty years. The restlessness and the hunger from my past life was pulling at me again. I needed things to remain the same, too much was changing things were moving way to fast. I was not in control any longer. I was losing both of my girls, and it was more that I could bear. The girls don't listen to me like they did in the past; they don't need me anymore. Why don't they understand that they are all I have?

The sign up ahead read Memphis eighty miles. I promised myself I would never come back to this place again. I closed the door on that part of my life for good, when I put Lady Bee in that nursing home. That part of my life was burned right along with Lady Bee's house.

Just saying that name, Lady Bee, sent chills down my spine. I missed my old friend. She was there for me when I needed her, but I needed her to let me go. I could not take that life any longer. I lived in that house with her male customers coming in and out for four years. I had to do something, or I would never have been free. After I had put her in the home, I started writing to her. I continued writing for a few years after I left her at the home, but I could not risk the girl's father finding out about my other life. Lots of good that did, me keeping my secret quiet, it's ironic when you think about it. The girl's dad ran off with a hooker he met at a bar. If only he had known he had been sleeping with one for twelve years.

Memphis 30 miles. I hated these darn road signs; they reminded me of just how close I was to my past sins. I have prayed a thousand prayers for forgiveness for my past life.

It didn't help. I wondered if Lady Bee was still alive. I whispered a prayer, God please let that old lady hang on until I can get there. I have to see her one more time. I can't continue to live with the guilt and shame of what I did to her.

Nothing will help until I see Lady Bee and beg her forgiveness.

It was almost 6:00 am on Wednesday morning. I drove all night. With any luck, I would be back home by Friday afternoon. I didn't want to take advantage of Ms. Lena's graciousness.

When I finally got there, I found a cheap hotel not too far from the nursing home where I left Lady Bee. I should have called the nursing home to make sure she was still there. But I realized I couldn't take the news over the phone if she weren't still alive. I had to see for myself.

I got settled in the hotel room. I didn't bring a lot with me. I lay my purse on the bed as I continued to put my things away. When I moved my other belonging on the bed, my purse fell off. My wallet fell open to the pictures of my daughters. As I looked at those pictures, I realized I was doing all this for them.

I hated leaving town without telling the girls where I was going. I knew they would worry and probably come looking for me, at least I hoped they would. Thelma is so preoccupied with her new fiancée she probably won't even notice I'm gone. Marie is probably too busy with this latest mess. I hate our relationship is so strained, and she doesn't feel that she can talk to me. I knew something was wrong when she started staying away all night. Lying to me like I don't know she is running after some no good man. If only she would talk to me.

The drive from Claxton was getting the best of me. I set the clock on the nightstand to wake me at 10:00. I needed a couple hours of sleep before I had to go and face my past. The tiredness finally took over as I drifted off to sleep.

The alarm went off at 10:00 am just like it was supposed to do. I pushed the clock to the floor and turned over and went back to my dream. I couldn't remember the last time I slept so soundly.

I finally got out of bed around noon. I took a hot shower. It was therapy for my body. I thought about eating down in the hotel, but the prices on the menu said that wasn't a good idea.

I wanted to save as much of the money Ms. Lena gave me as possible. I would never have imagined she would give me money for my trip.

I thought about calling the girls, but I knew there would be a great deal of questions that I was not prepared to answer. I headed for the old neighborhood.

Memphis wasn't the way I remembered. Everything was different. If memory served me, the nursing home should be only a few blocks away. It should be on the left-hand side, but there were apartments and condos everywhere.

I continued driving down the busy street praying something would start looking familiar. Fear was getting the best of me as I passed store after store. I was about to give up when I saw the sign up ahead. The nursing home was now a retirement village. Thank God they had not changed the name.

It was well after three with I arrived. I parked close to the entrance. I had no intention of staying any longer than necessary. Anxiety was creeping in, what the heck was I doing? Let sleeping dogs lie, whoever said that had to have been in a situation similar to mine.

The smell of bar-b-que greeted me as I walked into the lobby of the retirement village. The lobby was huge, with a large skylight in the middle. I stood in the middle of the lobby under the skylight and gazed up at the sunlight. It was as if God was waiting for me to speak to him. God I know you are with me. Give me the right words to say. I was so involved in my thoughts I didn't see the gray-haired figure in the wheelchair coming toward me.

"Honey do you see him too?" The small, frail voice spoke quietly.

"I'm sorry miss are you talking to me?"

"Well I guess I am, you are the only one looking up and talking to the man in the skylight. It's Okay I talk to him too. You know the man you were just talking too. I come here every day, and we have a nice little conversation. I ask him every day to take me home away from this place. The answer is always the same it's not time."

"Don't you like living here?"

"It's Okay, the people and the staff are nice enough. I don't want to die here. What family I have, have all forgotten about me. My grandson was visiting for a while, and then he got married and the new wife put a stop to that.

I'm sorry I'm running off at the mouth as usual. My name is

Dorothy, but everybody calls me Dot. Are you here visiting someone?"

"Yes, ma'am I am here visiting a very old friend. Her name is Beatrice. Maybe you have met her?"

"Goodness gracious! Are you Bee Bee's friend? She talks about you all the time. She has been expecting you. She said you would be coming for her any day. Bee Bee lives across the hall from me. We have been neighbors for years."

"Miss Dot I'm sure you must be mistaken. I have not seen my friend "Bee" in almost twenty years and."

"It doesn't matter she said you were her closest friend. You did use to work for her when she owned her own business didn't you?"

I stood speechless unable to move. Finally, I managed to shake my head in agreement.

"She said you left town when she closed the business."

The four halls in the lobby felt as though they were moving toward me. I couldn't breathe. I wanted to run for the exit. I needed to get out of there.

"Dear why don't you sit down on that bench over there? You don't look so good."

"No, I'm alright. I need to be going. I need some fresh air."

"You mean you came all this way to leave now? Why don't you walk down to the pool? We are having bar-b-que today. You do want to see Bee Bee don't you? Every Wednesday she's down by the pool beating the crap out of anyone who is fool enough to play cards with her. Besides you didn't come all this way to see your friend and leave without seeing her, which would be such a shame."

"Yes I guess it would be, but you don't understand our situation...."

"Shhh, you be quiet. None of that matters your friend has been waiting for years. It is time you talked to her."

"Thank you, Ms. Dot, it was nice talking to you. I will keep you in my prayers."

As I walked along the long hallway, I glanced over my shoulder for one last look at Dot. She had returned to the conversation with the man in the ceiling. I hoped he heard me as well.

I walked down the long hall in a daze. I had no idea what I would say to Lady Bee when I saw her. My heart was racing, and my palm were sweating. What if I have driven all this way and she hasn't forgiven me. I leaned up against the wall to keep my balance. I should have turned around and gone back to the car when I had the chance.

Coming back here was a foolish idea. To think I could turn back time and gain Lady Bee's forgiveness after everything I had taken from her.

"Ma'am are you alright? Do you need me to get you a chair or a glass of water? You don't look well at all."

"No thank you that won't be necessary, but thank you so much for your kindness."

It was time for me to go and face the music. I had come this far, and there was no turning back. I felt like I was doing the death walk of a condemned man. …*Yea, thou I walk through the valley of the shadow of death, I will fear no evil: cause thou art with me.* Thank you, Lord, I needed that.

21

The patio and grounds were covered. The residents were busy with various activities. The majority of the activity was near the rear of the yard by the edge of the pool. Residents were laughing, cheering, and clapping like they were at a football game.

If Lady Bee was involved, it would be just like her to be at the center of all the attention. I continued walking toward the crowd. A few of the older gentlemen began to move around, so I would have an opportunity to see the game.

As I drew near to the table, I caught a glimpse of the red flame that still burned on Lady Bee's head. It was her signature color. Her makeup was flawless as if chiseled by Michael Angelo himself. Accept for a few wrinkles here and there she looked exactly the same. The long sleeve white blouse covered the scars from the burns from years ago. The white blouse was crisp, clean, and white. The memory of the fire flooded my mind. The smell of the smoke filled my nostrils. I turned to leave when I heard that familiar voice; the voice that sent a chill down my spine.

"Well, Margie Girl are you going to stand there gawking all day, are do you plan on coming over here and saying hello?"

Tears welled up in my eyes. It was that voice her voice. The voice I dreaded hearing but thanked God it wasn't gone. I didn't prepare for this. "I did not want to disturb your game, Lad."

"It's just Bee Bee now Lady Bee died a long time ago. May she Rest in Peace. Grab a seat while I finish beating the crap out this attendant." Everyone continued cheering as Lady Bee or Bee Bee began clearing the money she had won from the table.

After a few moments, she stood and motioned for me to follow her to a set of chairs on the other side of the pool. When she stood, she grabbed a cane that was on the ground. She walked slowly by my side with a noticeable limp. I assumed I was staring at her limp.

"Had a stroke a few years back. Everything else is fine I guess the man upstairs wanted me to have a reminder of my stroke."

She quickly motioned for me to pull the chair away from the table and sit down.

"Well, Margie you look great. You look healthy. I can tell life has seasoned you a bit. Tell me, what's been happening with you since you dumped me here years ago?"

I tried to clear the dessert out of my throat before I spoke. I rehearsed the words to say to her in my mind for so many years. Now the words would not come. "Bee Bee you think I could get a glass of water I am suddenly very thirsty?"

"I guess you are thirsty you should certainly have a lot to say. I'll get an attendant to get you a bottle of water."

She raised her cane in the air and pointed to an ice chest. The attendant rushed over and handed her two bottles of water.

I took the bottle of water from her perfectly manicured hand. The silence between us was growing. I drank half the bottle of water. Without thinking I blurted out. "Bee Bee are you happy here; everyone seems very nice, and they're all so attentive."

"They are nice enough for hired help. So what is going on with you Margie? What finally brought you back to Memphis?"

I thought of countless ways to explain what I had done. Nothing seemed appropriate.

"I saw Francis a few days ago. You remember Francis don't you Bee. Francis was like a sister to me. I was in the grocery store. She had on the ring, Bee. Our ring. It's been years, but the ring was as familiar as the hair on my head. She had burns and scars on her face and arms. I wanted to say something to her, but guilt and shame got the better of me. I thought everyone got out of the fire safely Lady Bee. From the looks of Francis, I was wrong. I knew the good Lord was telling me it was time to right the wrong I did to you. Bee, I had to come back and say I'm sorry for leaving you here and never coming back to check on you. I was wrong. But there is something else I have to tell you…."

"You don't owe me any apologies. Life does what it wants when it wants."

"Please don't say anymore Lady Bee I have to tell you what happened the night of the fire. Please let me say this." I sat back in the chair and closed my eyes as I began to retell the events of that cold fall evening so many years ago. Lady Bee sat back in her chair and relaxed as if she had been waiting to hear this explanation for years.

"I tried telling you I wanted to leave. I guess I hoped you would figure it out. I would leave for hours at a time hoping that you would give my regulars to someone else. I couldn't stand another night of regular activities or another John.

I left around 6:00 that evening. I walked around the old neighborhood looking at people going and coming. I started walking back to the house when I recognized Lester's old blue Ford. He was waiting for me in front of the house. I hated the sight of that man.

I slipped around the back of the house and into the kitchen. I could hear you upstairs yelling at one of the Johns about what he owed. The doorbell rang. I knew it had to be Lester. I opened the basement door and ran downstairs. I hid in the corner of the basement. For the first time in my life, I prayed that God would give me a way out of this life. It was freezing in the basement. I went over to the furnace to get the fire going. I looked around for something to wrap around me. I intended to sleep in the basement if I had to. I found an old dirty blanket in the corner next to the furnace. I wrapped up and fell asleep as the furnace began to heat the basement.

I don't know how long I was asleep in the basement, it must have been a while; I was starving. I went up the stairs to the kitchen. The house was quiet there was no one in the kitchen the lights were out. The light from the stove clock showed 9:30. I needed to grab a sandwich and get back downstairs before one of the Johns decided to leave through the back entrance. I had the mustard and lunch meat in my hand. Lester came out of nowhere. He tapped me on the shoulder. I dropped everything on the floor. I ran as fast as I could for the basement door. Lester followed me down to the basement. When we got downstairs, he tried to throw me on the floor. He had been drinking, so it wasn't that hard to push him around. He just would not give up. He grabbed the blanket on the floor and tried to wrap it around me. I pushed him up against the furnace. The end of the blanket must have gotten too close to the flames. Before I could do anything, Lester was pushing me down and running for the stairs. I must have hit my head on something. I was in a daze for a few minutes. When I came to myself, the basement was engulfed in flames. I ran back upstairs to tell everyone to get out of the house. The fire was chewing the house in chunks.

When you and the other ladies finally heard me it was too late the fire was everywhere. I tried to get you out of the house, but you insisted on grabbing your things.

You were trying to get back to the kitchen. Part of the door facing came loose and hit you in the head. When I looked for you, you were lying on the floor your blouse was on fire. I put the fire out as best I could and dragged you to the door. Someone must have called the fire department; they helped me get you out. I tried to look around before I left the house. I screamed as loud as I could. I didn't hear anyone screaming or coming out the door. I assumed we got everyone out. But now I know Francis remained trapped upstairs. I rode with you to the hospital. I never looked back to see if the firemen had gone back to check for any survivors.

You awoke the next morning in the hospital. Over half of your body was covered in bandages. You kept asking what had happened to you. I thought it was perfect that you lost your memory. Everybody that came to see you told a different version of the story. I didn't think to ask about Francis, or anything else. I knew this was my chance to get away. I felt so badly for what I had done. I didn't have the nerve to tell you it was my fault you had lost your home. Please forgive me."

Lady Bee raised up in her chair. "You getting hungry? I hope that bar-b-que is done. These folks will starve an old women to death." "Lady Bee I mean Bee Bee didn't you hear a word I just said. I have held that secret for years."

"Do you feel better now that you got it off your chest?"

"Yes I do, is that all you have to say." With anger in my eyes.

"Didn't I tell you that life does what it wants when it wants to? It ain't nothing I can do about any of that now. I lost all those years with the best friend I ever had because you wasted time feeling guilty. Besides Lester found the Lord a few years after the fire. He found out where I was living. He came to visit me. His first question was where is Ms. Margie? The Lord said that was my wife. I told him to go back and ask the Lord to tell him where in the heck you were. He told me what he did to you that night that caused the fire. He asked me to apologize to you if you ever came to town. As for Francis and the other ladies in the house, I never heard a word from them.

Now, how much time are we going to waste talking? I hope you came to take me out of this place because that would be an answer to my prayers. I don't care where you live, it has got to be better than living here. Margie, they're only so much card playing a women can do."

Lady Bee stood up and grabbed her cane. She walked on ahead of me.

When she had gotten half way across the lawn, she looked back over her shoulder.

"Margie you did come to take me with you, didn't you since you did burn down my house?" She smiled the biggest smile I had ever seen and burst out laughing.

I didn't know how I would explain it to the girls, and at that moment it didn't matter. "Yes, Lady Bee I'm taking you home. I hope you don't still keep all that junk in your room the way you use to?"

After dinner, Lady Bee and I sat up in her room and talked until the staff told me I had to go. Lady Bee wanted me to spend the night. I think she was afraid that I wouldn't come back in the morning. If she only knew how good it felt to share everything I was going through with someone else. I told her all about the girls, and the situations they were involved in. She asked why I never remarried. I pretended I didn't hear the question.

It was after eleven when I got back to my room. I didn't realize how tired and stressed out I was until my head hit the pillow. I lay there in the darkness of the hotel room. Sleep refused to come. I needed to talk to my girls. Thelma should be at home by now unless she worked a double shift. At least that's the lie she tells me when she doesn't come home. It would be anybody's guess if Marie was there. I didn't feel like getting into it with her at this hour. I tossed and turned in bed until I realized I wouldn't be able to sleep until I had spoken to one of my girls, so it was no use putting it off.

I turned the lamp on. The receiver was in my hand. What was I going to tell them? How much should I get into over the phone?

"Hotel operator do you need me to help you make a call."

"No, ma am I'm sorry I think I can do it." I placed the receiver back in the headset. There was no reason for me to bother the girls tonight, all that would do is to make them worry. I'll wait until I have Lady Bee and I are on the road, I'll let them know we are on the way home.

Still no sleep. I had a bottle of aspirin in my purse. I popped a couple of pills and hit the pillow. The last thing I remembered seeing was Marie's face. I said a silent prayer for my child and drifted off into the most peaceful sleep I have had in years.

I felt a hundred percent better the next morning. I wanted to get over to the home in time for breakfast, but I didn't check out till after nine. I took one last look at the old neighborhood. Bee's old house was gone. I guess Bee forgot about the property, and the city built a new high-rise development.

I got over to the home around 10:30. It took Lady Bee forever to say goodbye to all of her friends.

The retirement village gave her a wonderful going away party. She struggled with leaving Ms. Dot. They had become close friends over the years. Finally, Lady Bee promised her that she would come back to get her as soon as she got settled in a place of her own. I didn't know how much truth it was to that story, but it seems to calm Ms. Dot's fear.

We shipped everything we couldn't get in the car on Greyhound. I had no idea where or how I was going to put all of her things. None of that seemed to matter at the time. All that mattered was that I had my best friend back and she was coming home with me.

Bee insisted on going over to the old neighborhood one last time.

"Great minds think alike. I came by the old neighborhood before coming to the home. The neighborhood looks great Bee. It would probably look even better if I weren't waiting to see Lester's old blue Ford drive around the corner at any minute."

Lady Bee asked me to park the car. We got out and strolled slowly down the block. In the middle of the block, she leaned on her cane.

"I did pretty well for myself after the fire Margie. I own all of this, the entire block. After I recovered from my burns, I got me a good attorney. I invested the insurance money from the fire. I kept the title to my land; then I bought the rest of the block. A few years later developers came along and wanted to develop this part of town. The Lord has been good to me. My investments have sustained me all these years. I'm telling you this cause I didn't want you to think that you will have to take care of me. I don't plan on being a burden to you Margie. I just want to be near my friend and die amongst you and your family."

We turned and began walking back toward the car. I remembered Lady Bee had a son, but she hadn't mentioned him.

"You know I have to ask. Where is your son?"

"I have no idea where he is. I get a post card from him every Christmas and maybe on my birthday.

He sent me a picture of my grandbabies a few years back. When he went off to that fancy school up north, he didn't want anything to do with me."

"Oh my, I don't know how you take it. I would die if I didn't know where my girls were."

"Why would I die when I ain't through living? Besides I'm his mother, he will need me way before I need him. Sooner or later he will call. I'm asking the good Lord to leave me here until he does. I left word at the retirement village to let him know that I was leaving. I gave them your name. He's some hot shot with the government if he want to he can find me."

"I'm sorry to hear that Lady Bee. Sometimes children don't understand the sacrifices we make for them."

"You talking about my situation or your own. I have no regrets about anything in my past. I keep telling you that life does what it wants when it wants. It's time we got on the road; I'm ready to move forward."

We left Memphis on Thursday afternoon. I hated driving at night. I was hoping to get us home before the girls made it in. Lady Bee wanted out of Memphis. She pointed her well-manicured finger at me.

"If you don't drive me out of this town right now, I'm going to take the wheel and drive myself."

"Lady Bee I didn't know you finally learned to drive."

"Who said anything about me learning to drive?"

I drove all evening and into the night. Lady Bee kept me awake with funny stories about the residents of the home. I know she hated more than anything to leave Ms. Dot. I know someday very soon we would have to make the trip back to pick up her old friend.

Claxton looked the same when we hit the city limits. But everything in my life was about to change. How would the girls feel about

Lady Bee living with us? I dreaded answering all their questions. It's none of their business anyhow, after all it is my house.

It was after 10:00 when we reached the neighborhood. Lady Bee asked me to take her to the grocery store to pick up a few things. I made her welcome to anything at my house. But she insisted on contributing to the grocery bill.

The store was quiet this late in the night. Lady Bee grabbed a shopping cart and attacked the store like a warrior going to battle.

"Bee what has gotten into you? You would think you are going to war the way you are attacking these isles."

"Do you know how long it has been since I have shopped for groceries? The home would take us to the grocery store, but it was a waste of time. They watched everything you put in the basket.

They reminded you about your diet on every isle of the store. I feel like a kid in a candy store."

Buying groceries has never been an adventure before. I haven't had that much fun going shopping in my entire life. Lady Bee insisted that I get the things I wanted, not just the things I needed. When we got to the register she, paid the entire bills. I asked to help her, but she insisted. It felt so good to have finally somebody to care about me for a change. I drove her around town for a while, until I stopped the car in front of my old house down by the river.

I parked the car in the driveway and told her we lived here before the flood a few years ago. It's been my dream to come back to this house one day. This house belonged to my mother. I feel close to her when I am here. We didn't get out. We sat there for a while and talked about the repairs I would like to have done on the house. Bee listened and asked a few questions about the remaining houses on the block. I could tell she was getting tired, so I drove her to the house.

Marie and Thelma hadn't made it home when we arrived; which was a prayer answered. We unpacked the car. I placed the majority of Bee's things in my bedroom. The remainder of the stuff would be stacked on the back porch until we could figure out what to do with it.

I offered my room to Bee, but she insisted on sleeping on the couch. I told her that it would only be for a few months. When Thelma marries the doctor, I'm sure he has a mansion already built and ready for her to go in.

"Margie you are going to have to let that go. Kids grow up. They have to go on and find their way in life. Besides it's time you got your life."

"Well, Bee I have my life. I have a job, my church and."

"Yea that's about all you have. You don't have anything for you. That's a crying shame. I tell you now that is going to change. We are going to start living. I ain't never heard it said that there was a sin in living a happy life. You have just forgotten how to go about doing it."

"I don't know what you think you are going to change about my life. I like things just the way they are. Good night Lady Bee I will see you in the morning."

22

Thelma

It was nice having a quiet dinner with my kid sister. I hated seeing her so unhappy. Especially when I have so much happiness with CJ. She looks as though she has the weight of the world on her shoulder. Why won't she talk to me about what is going on with her? We were never really close, but I hope she knows that I would always be there for her. My happiness would be so much more meaningful if I knew my sister has some joy in her life.

"I had a wonderful evening. I can't wait for the day when you take me to our house babe."

"It won't be long Thelma just a few more months. I'm hoping that your mother would have come around by then. Look Thelma isn't that your mother's car in the yard. Looks like she's back from her trip."

"I wonder where she could have been that she could not have called to at least let us know that she was alright."

"I'm not coming in Thelma. I think it would be best if you and your mother had some time alone. Try not to be too upset with her. You'll never know what she's going through, and it's just wasn't time to let you and Marie in on the secret."

I kissed this gorgeous caring man good evening. I didn't want to get into any arguments with Mama, not after the wonderful evening I had with my marvelous fiancée. All I'm going to do is go in and kiss Mama good night and tell her how much I have missed her."

"You know you can call me anytime day or night if you need to talk. I love you, Thelma."

"I love you too. Drive safely. Are you on early duty tomorrow?"

"Yeah I am in the ER tomorrow morning. Friday mornings are always rough I guess folks have too much Thursday night. Good night sweetheart I will see you in the morning.

The light in the living room was still on, which was very unusual for this time of night. Mama was probably sitting up waiting for me and Marie. I guess it's finally time to tell us where she has been.

I really should have found my keys before I got out of the car with CJ. Where are those darn keys?

"Come on in child, it don't look like you're going to find those keys."

"Excuse me, ma'am. Where is my mother and what are you doing in our home at this hour?"

"Aren't you going to come in? I need to close the front door, the bugs and mosquitos are setting up camp. My name is Bee. I'm your last remaining cousin on your grandmother's side. Have a seat you mother is taking a bath she will be right out."

"Glad to meet you, Bee, my name is Thelma. I'm sorry I have never heard Mama speak of a Cousin Bee. Where did you say you were from?"

"I didn't say where I was from, but since you asked, I'm from Memphis. But I can talk to you about that in the morning. I'm kind of tired. Good night Thelma. Sleep well I'll see you in the morning."

"Cousin Bee I wouldn't count on getting much sleep. My sister, Marie will be coming in in just a few minute. I know she will have a thousand questions. She's not the type to wait until the morning."

"Thank you for the warning, but I am not the type to stay awake when I said I'm going to bed."

This situation was becoming more and more bizarre by the minute. I went to my room and closed the door. I knew the fireworks would resume the minute Marie stepped foot in the living room and saw a strange woman sleeping on our couch.

I was undressed and in bed when I heard Mama emerge from the bathroom. She went to the living room to make sure Cousin Bee was comfortable. I could tell they were whispering about something, but I couldn't make out what was being said. When they were finished talking, she peeked her head in my room. I could tell she was trying to determine if I was already asleep. I had had enough excitement for one day. I closed my eyes and didn't acknowledge her presence.

"Thelma I know you're not asleep. You don't have to say a word. I will talk to you in the morning before you leave for work. Cousin Bee will be living with us. I know your grandmother would be pleased that we helped our relatives out. You sleep well."

I guess she got the hint that I had nothing to say to her. She closed the door on her way out.

I turned over and drifted off to sleep. The bed still smelled of CJ. The memory of the evening enveloped me like a quilt.

I was in his arms again when. I heard Marie put her key in the door. I jumped out of bed and got my robe.

When I stepped in the hallway, I heard Marie.

"Excuse me, ma'am. Who the heck are you and why are you sleeping in our living room, on our sofa?"

Mama heard Marie's voice and rushed into the hallway. "Well, Marie you decided to come home finally? Marie I would like you to meet your Cousin Bee. She will be living with us. Would you mind showing some manner and greeting her?"

"Hello Mama, I'm glad to see you made it back home safely, even though you worried us half to death when you left and didn't say a word. Who is this guess in our home? I don't recall you ever mentioning a cousin. Where has she been living? Why is she living with us? It's not like we have a whole lot of room for sharing."

Cousin Bee was finally awake and from the looks of things she was ready to deal with whatever Marie had to dish out.

"Well you, must be Marie. I have heard a lot about you. My name is Bee. I am your last remaining cousin on your grandmother's side.

As your mother said I will be staying with you for a while, until I find a suitable place of my own. I trust you don't have a problem with that. Not that it matters if you do. Your mother invited me. Now if you don't mind you are in my bedroom and, I am ready to go back to sleep. That is what people do at this hour. If you have any more questions for me, I will gladly answer them for you in the morning."

Marie was practically fuming.

"Well, Mama don't you have anything to say?"

Mama looked casually at me, and then to Cousin Bee. "Well, Marie I think you have said enough for one night. Sleep well we will talk in the morning."

Cousin Bee turned the light out in the living room, which left Marie standing in the dark with no one to talk too. She stomped past my room and walked to her room and slammed the door.

It was well after midnight when the house settled down. But it was just the calm the before the storm. Marie was ready for a fight, and she would be ready for Cousin Bee in the morning.

23

Marie

I didn't know who this Cousin Bee person was? But she had better get ready for a change in her attitude. She is not going to talk to me that way in my house. I don't understand why Mama thinks she can bring people home to live with us, and not have the decency to ask even our opinion. It's not like Thelma, and I don't live here too. I'll have something to say about that in the morning. This house is becoming a zoo. Mama is taking in every stray that comes through needing a home. I can't wait to get out of here. I don't recall her ever mentioning a long lost cousin on my grandmother's side. It's something not quite right about all of this.

I don't have time for all this nonsense. I have to get the rest of the delivery for James. God I could kill him for all this added stress. I'll probably never get to sleep. I wish I could just turn back time and go back to a year ago when things were much easier.

The full moon was smiling in my bedroom window. I wish I could stay in this bed forever.

God if you still listen to me I could use your help. I know you are aware of the situation. I know by now Mama has your attention, but if you could, please help me get out of this mess with James. I'm not going to make a lot of promises that you know I can't keep, but I will try to get along with Mama, and Cousin Bee. Thanks for listening.

James will not win. He will not get the better of me. I am going to go into that store in the morning and get the remainder of his order. Then I am going to call him and set up a time to meet him. James and this mess will be over soon.

The alarm clock screamed at me around 6:00. Getting out of the bed was the last thing in the world I wanted to do. After hitting snooze for the second time I rolled out of bed. What is that noise? Who the heck is that yelling in the hall? Oh my God! It must be that Cousin Bee person. Where the heck has she be living; on a farm.

That's the first thing I'm getting straight this morning. This house is not a farm, and you are not a rooster doing your duty in the morning.

Lord have mercy. There she goes again,

"Y'all planning on sleeping all day. I thought when folks had jobs to go to they had to be up moving about!"

I rolled out of my room and slid into the bathroom. When I came out Mama, and her cousin were perched like pigeons on a line at the table.

"Good morning Marie, would you like me to get you a cup of coffee?"

"No Mama that won't be necessary, since Cousin Bee has the whole house up I may as well get my cup of coffee. While I'm on the subject Cousin Bee, I hope you don't plan on waking up the household with your screaming every morning."

"Good morning Ms. Marie, I'm sorry did I wake you? I just thought when people have jobs they are supposed to get up and ready to move so they can be on time. I got up at 5:00 and made breakfast for you and your mother. But if you aren't hungry I can sleep late like everybody else."

"I didn't say I wasn't hungry. The breakfast looks great. I just don't think we need a drill sergeant this early in the morning to get us out of bed."

"I will try to remember that Marie. Would you like for me to fix you a plate? We have eggs, bacon, and pancakes."

"Thank you I would love the bacon and pancakes. So Cousin Bee where have you been living?"

"I have been living in a retirement village in Memphis. I contacted your mother and asked her if I could come and live out my last days with my family."

"So you don't have any other family that you could have stayed with, not that I am saying you are not welcome."

"Oh, I know you would never want a guest to feel unwelcome Marie. Yes, I do have other family, but I was always close to your grandmother. Your mother is like my daughter."

"So where is the rest of your family...?"

"Marie don't you think you need to hurry up and finish those pancakes. I know you have to get to the store?

"I guess I should eat and get a move on I have to take care of a few things before the store opens. We'll continue our discussion at a later date, Cousin Bee."

"I can hardly wait dear. Would you like some more coffee?" Cousin Bee smiled at me with that fake plastered smile on her face. I know it's something more to this story. I will get to the bottom of this.

I finished with breakfast and said my goodbyes to our house guest and Mama. Thelma was still asleep she didn't have to go in until noon.

It was a beautiful day. The sun was coming up. The river gleamed and turned as I drove across the bridge. I got to work around 7:30. Usually, there's no-one around accept the night crew.

They're usually finishing up last minute stocking. I needed to get the clothes and shoes and put them in my car. I didn't want to explain to Cathy was I was doing.

I hid my stash of clothing in the women's wear department. Everything was just as I left it. Now it was time to get to the shoe department and get the shoes. There were only a few members of the night crew stocking the shelves.

The door was slightly ajar. I heard voices coming from the rear of the room. I couldn't take the chance being seen, so I moved to the left toward the corner. The back door of the stock room was open. Cathy along with the man from the white car and the floor manager were talking in the doorway. Cathy was busy pointing to boxes of shoes that she stacked around the wall. The men were inspecting the boxes. I tried to get closer to hear the conversation. The man from the white car moved closer to the open door. He pointed to the large dumpster in the rear of the parking lot. My mind flashed back to the day Cathy was in the car with the man. They were interested in the dumpster on that day as well. What could Cathy possibly be doing with the store manager and this other strange man? I didn't want to know anything else about this situation. It was clear Cathy was hiding something from me. I hope she hasn't got herself into a situation that she can't fix. Cathy would have to get herself out of this mess.

I need to get my shoes and get the heck out of here. Cathy placed the shoes on the end of the rack in the corner. My hands were a bit wobbly; as I tried reaching for the shoes without removing the boxes near them. Boxes fell to the floor. In an instance the strange man scooted out the door, the floor manager headed for the exit, and Cathy strolled over to the shelf where I was trying to pick up the boxes.

"Girl what are you doing in the stock room this early? I would have brought your shoes to you."

"Well, Cathy I would hate to bother you. You look like you have a situation that you have to take care of yourself."

"What are you talking about I'm not in any situation."

"Oh, yeah. So I guess it's normal for you to be in the stockroom on a Friday morning with the store manager and a strange man in a white Chevy."

"I was just showing Mr. Foster the new line of shoes."

"Please don't bother to lie to me Cathy, I thought we were better friends than that.

What you do is your business. I certainly am in no position to judge you. I guess we both have got to learn to trust each other a lot more."

"Marie I know how this must look to you. I wish I could fill you in on everything in time, I will tell you everything. Until then, all I can say is please don't think the worst of me until you have all the facts. Please give me the benefit of the doubt and trust our friendship."

"Whatever Cathy, I need to get out on the floor."

"Marie I would appreciate it if you wouldn't tell anyone what you saw in the stock room this morning. Believe me it won't be long before everything comes to a head, then everything will make sense."

"You don't have to worry Cathy your little secret is safe with me. But you know that goes both ways. I need you to trust me as well."

"Marie I know you are in some situation with that James guy you just met. If you would just talk to me, I know people that can help you." Cathy looked concerned.

"I'll see you later Cathy I have to get out on the floor."

Stacy was standing guard at my register when I arrived.

"Good morning, Marie I was getting worried that you may not have made to work. Did you take care of all your business? Did you get everything you needed?"

"Yes, Stacy I still have a few minutes before the store opens, but I need to run to my car to drop off these packages." I kept wondering to myself, why is it that my business is suddenly her business?

"Of course I understand you go ahead I will get your register open for you."

The bags of clothes and shoes were heavy, but I managed to get everything into the trunk and get back to the store. Stacy was standing at the register with a big grin on her face when I returned. She was beginning to get on my nerves.

"The store is probably going to be busy today. Let me know if you need anything." Stacy was grinning like she had won the lottery.

"Yeah, I will Stacy you have a great day. Since I opened up, I really would like to be out of here by five."

"That shouldn't be a problem. I'll talk to you later."

The day was turning out to be more that I could handle. First Cathy with her secretive behavior and now Stacy acting like her and I are the best of friends. I wanted more than anything for this day to be over, but I still had to call James to get the drop-off instructions. I was dreading that call.

The store was a madhouse as usual. I avoided Cathy and Stacy like the plague. She must have asked me three times if I wanted to have lunch. I hated to be rude, but I just didn't want anything to do with her. Around 4:45 the store finally calmed down. I closed out my register, gathered my things, and ran to the ladies room to hide. I knew James would be expecting me to call him at 5:00 on the dot, I had no intention of being late. I had to make sure I had access to the pay-phones in the break room before the 5:00 o'clock shift change.

The room was empty, thank God. The phone was in my hand. I wanted so badly to tell James to stick it where the sun doesn't shine, but I couldn't risk him hurting my loved ones. Why was it necessary for the phone to ring so many times, it's not like he didn't know it was me.

"Hey Pretty Lady, I guess you finally realized that I mean business when I say call me on time. I assume you have all the items I asked about in the sizes that I asked for?"

"Yes, James I have everything that you asked me to get. I can drop them off this evening on my way home. I want this to be over and done with."

"Not so fast girl. This operation ain't over till I say it's over. So you may as well relax and enjoy the ride, cause saying its over is not even in my vocabulary. I have other things to do this afternoon. So you will meet me tomorrow just as I planned. Now you get a piece of paper and write down this address. I need you to be there tomorrow at 1:00 on the dot. I do believe you are off tomorrow so it shouldn't be a problem for you to be there and be on time. You ready, you got that paper like I told you?"

"Yeah, James I'm ready. James, I am not a rich woman I don't know how you expect me to continue to furnish you and your women with clothes."

"Like I told you that is not my problem. You obviously have tapped into some well of wealth. If you know what's good for you, you will keep coming up with the money you need to get the things I want. The address you're coming to tomorrow is 1256 Wesley Ln. Apt 224."

"I've heard of Wesley Ln. It's on the south side of Franklin. That's a pretty rough neighborhood. Couldn't we meet someplace else, like a park or even the club where we met?"

"I don't believe I stuttered when I gave you the address, and I know you are not hard of hearing. I said I want you on Wesley Ln at 1:00." The phone when dead.

I picked up my purse and other belongings and walked quietly to my car. As I drove out of the parking lot, I could see Cathy exiting the back door. I could tell she wanted to ask me for a lift home.

I'm so glad she got the hint and didn't try to flag me down. Talking to Cathy was the last thing on my mind.

The drive across the bridge did nothing to calm my nerves or my fears. James had his claws in me, and he had no intention of letting me go. Lord, what am I going to do? I can't tell Mama or Thelma they would just worry themselves to death. If only I had someone to talk to that understood my situation.

Lord if you haven't given up on me please send me someone to talk too. I would hate if James did something to me and there was nobody that knew what going on.

I drove up the driveway to the house. Mama and Cousin Bee were sitting on the porch. Getting into it with them was the last thing on my little mind. If only I can get past the two of them.

I went to grab my things from the back seat of the car when I heard the house phone ring. Mama got up and went back inside the house. Now all I had to do was get passed this old lady.

"Child whatever his name is he is running you through the ringer."

"Excuse me, Cousin Bee are you talking to me?"

"I guess I am since ain't nobody else out here, but the roaches and mosquitoes."

"I don't know what you are talking about and I am too tired to try to explain anything to you."

"You don't need to explain anything Marie. You just need to come clean to somebody about all that stuff that's going on in your head. Baby, your head is going to explode. I am a real good listener, and I have been known to solve a problem or two."

"I wish it were that easy. If talking to you or anybody else would clear up this mess I have to deal with believe me I would gladly spill my guts."

"Marie I know how to keep my mouth closed. We wouldn't have to worry your mother. It would be between me and you."

"Why would you want to help me with anything? You don't even know me. Besides I don't even know if I like you yet; I know I don't trust you."

"I've known lots of other young girls like you Marie. When it's all said and done, they all wish they had someone in their corner that they could trust. Just know that I am here when you are ready to talk."

"Don't sit out here too long Cousin Bee the mosquitoes can get pretty fierce. I'll see you in the morning."

24

James

It's hot as hell riding around in this car. Dam air conditioner would quit in the summer. Here I am out in this heat having to check on these silly whores this early in the morning. I can't have them slacking off they'll start thinking they're running something. If they know what's good for them, they had better be out here making my money. What time is it anyhow? I need to check in on that fool I got in the store. She should be opening up by now. I hope she ain't doing all that darn talking cause I'm not about to stand in this heat just to talk to her.

There's a pay phone on the next corner; this darn cell phone ain't worth a quarter. Darn thing works when it wants too.

"Damn the phone just ringing. Where the hell is she?"

"Hello, Wilson Fine Clothing. How may I help you?" The operator had to locate that fool before she came to the phone.

"Hey baby how's my girl doing today?"

"Hey, James I was just thinking about you. Baby, I've been waiting for your call."

"How is everything going in the store this morning? I talked with Marie yesterday, so I know she has all my stuff. I would have hated to have to make it clearer to her."

"No baby your new girl is doing just fine. She was late getting back from lunch the other day. When she did come back, she had a wad of money. She went in and took care of your order.

Baby you are going to be quite pleased with the new stuff she's bringing you. I made sure she had time to pick out everything you needed in all the right sizes. She opened the store yesterday. I wanted to give her time to get your order together."

"That's my girl; I knew I could count on you. I got to run. We'll talk later."

"Wait a minute baby. Now that you got all you need on Marie, it's time you take care of me. I mean take care of me in that special way that only you can."

"Be patience girl, you know I got you. I got something special planned for you and me after I get Marie in check with her regular deliveries. You continue to keep an eye on her. Do you know if she has been talking to anyone about our little arrangement?"

"No, I don't think so. One think is strange, baby the way she just came up with all that money. Hell, we don't get paid until next week. We both know she ain't got no rich uncles. I can't think of anyone that works in this store that has that kind of money before pay day.

"Yeah, you sound like you may have something there, I got to go, keep me up to date. I'll holler at you later."

Glad I got that fool covered. OK, Pretty Lady is doing just fine. She will deliver on schedule. She is going to learn a thing or two about messing with a real man. By the time I'm through with her, she and her Mama will be calling for Michael and all his angels to get them out of this mess.

Everything would be just perfect if I didn't have to deal with that fool in the store. That's the last think I want to do is spend time with her and her whining. I have to be cool. I got to have her in that store even though she is getting on my nerves. When I get through with her she will be out like yesterday's trash. All she has to do is shut up and keep an eye on my Pretty Lady.

Whew what is this? Somebody stop the damn drums in my heads! Another one of those damn headache. These things are getting worst. Where are those damn pills? All that talking didn't help either. Need to go to a doctor about this, but I just need a little more

136 | Denise Montgomery

money and little more time, and all this will be over. I can let these whores and all the rest of this trash behind me. I'll move back north and start a new life.

I need to go by the place and get myself straight. A drink would be really good about now. Everything would be perfect if I didn't have to go back and deal with that lazy ass, Liz. I know she's been sitting up all day eating and drinking beer like she owns something. It probably ain't one damn beer in the house. I need to get a few things straight with her. Liz is becoming a liability, with that big mouth of her. She's going to spoil everything for me. What good is she anyhow? All she does all day is sit around and eat. If she gets any bigger, I may have to put her on the street to earn her keep. I should have left her with that fool she was living with anyhow. She'd be dead by now, the way he was beating the crap out of her.

She just like all the rest of these whores. Come to think of it I could probably get a few dollars off of her if I put her on the street.

I just got to keep myself focused. I can't let anything get under my skin. Damn! It's hot in this car. It's time for an upgrade. I got to have some air. I need to get these stupid women working on the money for my next car. Okay, everybody is in place all my corners are covered.

The stroll was looking pretty good this morning. Everything just right. It's cool on the street. My women know they better be in place or they know what's coming next. Yeah, they all working just like they're supposed to. Now it's back to the crib.

I can't wait to get the hell out of this neighborhood. I hate these apartments. Everybody down here is waiting for hand-outs and hanging on the corners. I don't deserve to live like this. I'm sick of looking at these whores on the corner and the wine-os on the street. This damn place is full of rats and roaches. I got to get out of here. I need just a little more time.

Please let it be a parking space by the door. I ain't parking my car on the back side. That's for real. These fools are waiting to see what they can steal. To hell with that.

That darn TV blasting through the door again. I know I've told Liz a thousand time. I know she don't need no damn hearing aids. Why everybody in the place got to hear what she's looking at on TV. The place is probably hot and nasty. Ain't no need in knocking, forget about using the key, it's like a darn grocery store. Liz sits up with the door open. Anybody that was coming by can get an eye full of my business. Like I said the damn door is wide open. Where the hell is everybody?

"Liz where the hell are you? Come out the kitchen, you been in there all day. Where the hell are those other two? They should be back by now. Girl look at you. You keep gaining all this weight. I'm warning you; I'm gone put you on the street. The exercise will do you good."

"Whatever James. You gave your girls big orders to fill this time. It takes more time to steal all that stuff and not get caught."

"Well now ain't that just real motherly of you. You act like you give a crap about them two. Frankly I hope they do get caught. I would have room for some fresh meat. Lisa and Dee Dee are just a little bit too comfortable. I'm going to up their orders. But now I need to talk to you. I need you to listen real *good*. Wait just a minute I need to get a beer. Is there any left before I walk over to the fridge? I won't be surprised if it's not."

"James I didn't drink all your beer. I got better sense than that. I get lonely and depressed all day in this house by myself. What else am I supposed to do other than drink your beer?"

"Well, I can think of a couple of things you could do Liz. Number one, you could get a job. Number two if you don't want a job you can go out and steal like the other two. If you want to help, I can line you up with a John tonight. But one thing is for certain, you are going to shut your big mouth! You had no business telling Marie anything. I got a good thing going. You're about to mess it up."

"I didn't tell her nothing, but the truth about you little brother. *You are a user.* You have used women all your life."

"It's mighty funny you didn't mind me using women when I got you away from that fool you was living with that was beating the crap out of you. You know anytime you get tired of living here.

"I think you know I can't leave James. I don't have nowhere to go. I appreciate you keeping a roof over my head. I just hate what you are doing to these women. James, it just ain't right. You start out with them stealing for you. When they can't steal anymore, you put them on the street. When is enough, enough? You said that when you had your money saved that we would leave Franklin and move away and start all over."

"Like I said Liz anytime you want to leave there is the door. As for me, I'm done with these silly women when I say I am. I'm tired of talking to you about this. My head is killing me? I need something to drink. Get the hell up and get me a can of beer. Where did you say Lisa and Dee Dee were? It don't take all day to go hit a store and get back with the stuff." The chair by the door looked like it was miles away. I need to sit down.

"Well, James did you ever think that one time they may get caught trying to steal?"

"No, for your information I don't think about them getting caught. Cause I really could care less. That's their problem. They know they better come back here with my stuff. Or they can make my money the old fashioned way. I'm getting tired of your whining and complaining. I can find a replacement for you too." The room was moving in circles. The pain was becoming unreal. Dam it Liz wasn't helping the situation at all.

"That won't be necessary James. You are leaving already. Where are you on your way?"

Damn, my head is hurting. Rubbing it ain't helping a bit. I need to get away from Liz before I hurt her. "I'm getting as far away from you as possible. I need to look at something new and fresh, so I guess I'll be going over to the stroll today. It's time for some fresh meat. If anybody calls, you would be wise to keep your mouth shut, or you are going to need a pair of comfortable shoes to stroll down 5th street. It's up to you I don't mind introducing you to a few of my old friends.

By the way, I want this place cleaned up by the time I get back. Marie, the one you have been blabbing all my business to will be here at 1:00 o'clock today. I should be here when she arrives, but just in case I'm a little late I don't want you saying anything to her. Since we don't live in a barn, get up and lock the door when I leave.

Damn I still didn't get my beer. I ain't going back in there with Liz. I got to figure out something to do with her. She ain't worth the trouble she's causing me.

I need to find Lisa and Dee Dee. I'm raising their orders. The sooner they get caught, the sooner I'll have room for some new meat.

I can't wait till Pretty Lady can't fill her first order. I'll have her out on the stroll so fast she won't know what hit her. I got the perfect John for her. He can have her after I take care of her first. I'll have her on the corner by the end of the summer. Damn, I'm good. Just thinking about that made my head feel a whole lot better.

Let me go and check on a few things, so I can be back here by 1:00.

25

The sun did its job and woke me up at 6:00 am. It was time get up and deal with the situation at hand. I rolled out of bed, grabbed my robe, and pushed my hair out of my face. Thelma was busy fixing toast and coffee. She looked so happy and peaceful.

"Good morning, Marie it's been ages since the last time I spoke with my sister. She threw a bride's magazine on the table in front of me. I don't have to work today. I thought that maybe we could go and look at wedding dresses if you have the time?"

"I'm sorry Thelma I know I promised you that I would help with planning the wedding, but my schedule is hectic right now. Maybe we could get together next week."

"Marie you only have one big sister, and if you think for one moment that I am going to let you get out of helping me plan this wedding, girl you are sadly mistaken. As soon as you have your schedule for next week, you are going to give me a date and time that we can start to work on this wedding. As for now, you need to go back to bed for a bit you look horrible. Or I can I fix you some breakfast?"

"No, I'm not in the mood for breakfast, but thanks for letting me know I look like hell."

"Marie you know you can tell me if you are going through something. I am always here for you."

Tears were welling in the corners of my eyes. I had to get out of here. "Thelma you know I love you and I wish you the best of luck with CJ, please don't ever forget that. I promise as soon as I can I will give you a free day. I have to go and get dressed I have a lot of errands to run."

At that moment, all I wanted to do was get back in bed and cover my head, and pray that life would get better.

The minute my head hit the pillow there was a knock at the door. Who the heck is knocking on my door this early in the morning? Before I even had a chance to respond, the door was open. Cousin Bee was standing in my room looking like the Wicked Witch of the West, with flaming red hair.

"Excuse me I didn't get the chance to respond before you came barging in my room."

"Well, would you like for me to go out and come back in to give you a chance to respond? Would you feel better?

I don't stand on that formal stuff child; we are all female, and we are in this thing together."

"What do you want Cousin Bee since you are already in my room?"

"I overheard you telling Thelma that you were off today. I really would like to go into town. I need just a few things from the store. I know you have things planned, but I would pay you for your time. I don't want to bother your mother. She's going to work for Mrs. Larson today. I guess she feels guilty cause she took those few days off coming to get me. Can you help me out? It won't take, but a minute to get dressed."

I knew I would probably never hear the end of the matter from Mama if I didn't help our relative out. I didn't have to meet James until 1:00 that would give me something else to focus my attention on. "Okay, I will be ready to leave at 9:00. I'm going to lie down for about another hour. Maybe I will look and feel a lot better."

"I'll be waiting on the front porch at 8:45, thanks again."

The extra hour of sleep didn't help a bit. I got dressed and walked out to the front porch. The Wicked Witch of the West was riding her broom and ready for travel when I stepped on the porch at 8:55. "Where would you like to go to pick up the items you need?"

"Well, I was hoping you could take me to a nice clothing store. I haven't had a chance to buy nice underwear in years. For some reason the home thought all old women wanted to wear old lady underwear. I want something pretty and frilly with lace on it."

"Is price a problem?" I said with a sly smile on my face.

"Sweetie if I didn't say cheap, that means I got the money. Are you ready to travel?"

My dear cousin is in for a treat. She'll think she has died and gone to heaven when I take her to work.

Wilson's has one of the best line of ladies lingerie this side of the Mississippi. It would be just my luck that noisy Cathy or even worst Stacy would see me with Cousin Bee dropping cash like she is made of money. I know a few stores in downtown Claxton, which would work just as well. It's not worth the risk.

"Well Cousin Bee the store where I work would probably have what you are looking for, but we don't have a lot of time, so I'll take you to a store in Claxton. I have an appointment at 1:00."

"Well don't you think we could get there and back by 11:00? I certainly wouldn't won't to make you late.

Ain't no use in fooling around in Claxton, if you know your store has what I need?"

"OK, you promise when I say it's time to go that you will be ready to go."

"Honey all you have to do is give me the look and I will be at the car before you."

I hated to admit it, but I was enjoying this old woman's company. We drove across the bridge and into town. Cousin Bee loved Franklin she said it reminded her of Memphis years ago.

We arrived at the store around 9:45. Cousin Bee was out the car in a flash. She attacked the store with a vengeance.

"Marie you don't have to watch over me. I want you to pick out a nice outfit that you have been wanting and find something for your mother and

Thelma as well. I want to show my appreciation. Don't worry about me sweetheart I'm not broke. I want you to pick out things that you and your family would like. How much time do I have?"

"Well Cousin Bee we need to leave around 11:00 to get you back, and I can make it to my meeting on time."

"Alright, Marie I will meet you back at this register at 11:00."

Cousin Bee disappeared into the throngs of shoppers. I figured this would be a good time to look for dresses for the various functions I'm sure Thelma would have before the wedding. It felt so good to be shopping for myself again. It didn't take long to find the perfect party dress for Thelma and me. I even had something nice for Mama, even though I doubted that she would wear it. I could have shopped all day.

The voice over the loudspeaker brought me back to reality, Marie Rhoades will you report to the front register. Why is the store calling me? I'm not at work today. It is after all my day off. I'm shopping for myself. I turned toward the front of the store with the dresses on my arm. The clock in the center of the store sounded 11:30. What the heck was I thinking? I have to get Cousin Bee back to the house and then back to town.

Cousin Bee was waiting patiently for me at the register when I arrived. She had already paid for her items and was ready to pay for mine. "Cousin Bee we don't have time. If you have your items, we really should be going."

"Girl put those things on the counter. We didn't come all this way for you to leave those pretty dresses here."

"You don't understand I can't be late for this appointment, my life depends on it. I have to get you home then back across town." Before I could say no she had ripped the dresses from my arm and placed them on the counter.

"Don't worry child we will get there in plenty of time. Even if you have to take me to the appointment with you."

We finished paying for the clothing. I ran to the car. It was 11:45. There was no way I could drop Cousin Bee off and get back to town by 1:00. "Cousin Bee I need you to keep your mouth shut about the place I'm about to take you. I don't need Mama and Thelma asking me a whole lot of questions that I really can't answer."

"I already told you I was a good listener. Whatever the trouble you have gotten yourself into, you are going to need someone to help you get out of it. Go ahead and drive to your appointment. If you need me to get down in the back seat, that won't be a problem. I just want to help you, Marie. This problem is getting to be a bit too much for you."

"You won't need to get down in the seat I don't think. I have to drop off a package at an apartment in a rough neighborhood. I didn't want to go to this neighborhood by myself, so in a way you are an answer to a prayer. I continued to drive out of the downtown area. I have never had an occasion to visit this side of Franklin. The only thing I knew about Wesley Ave. was what I heard on TV. There was nothing ever good said about this place. It didn't take long before the landscape changed. I knew I was in the right place.

"Do you have any idea where we are going, Marie? It's obvious that you don't hang out in this part of town. Why don't you pull up to the corner and I will ask for directions to the street? I'm sure if you give me his name someone probably knows where he hangs out or where he lives."

"Why would you think it's a man that I'm seeing? I never said anything to you about who I am meeting."

"Are we going to keep playing this game? Or do you plan on trusting me enough to tell me the truth about this mess you are in."

"I need a little more time. Would you please just ask the man on the corner where Wesley Ave is?" I pulled over to the curb, and Cousin Bee began a conversation with this strange man as if she had known him all her life. When she finished, she gave me the directions to Wesley Ave.

"You know Marie, all these folks down here are people just like you and me.

The only different between us and them is the choices they made. Nobody has ever told them that they could do better. Wesley Ave is the next corner. I don't know who this guy is that has you so scared, but if he is living down here child you are way out of your league."

We pulled into the apartment building. There were women and men standing out watching every move I made. Finally, I found the building where James lived. I saw his car parked in a space close to the building. I wanted to get this over with as fast as possible. Eyes followed me from every direction. I went into the trunk and grabbed all the bags. I should have made two trips, but there was no way that was going to happen. I leaned into the car to tell Cousin Bee I would be right back before I could say anything.

"What's the apartment number where you are going? If you aren't out of there in 15 minutes, I am coming to get you. I won't be coming alone."

"Please don't I don't want to make him angry. I promise I will be out in 15 minutes." I felt like a condemned man on his way to the death chamber. In a way that was true. The life I have known was slowly slipping away from me.

Cousin Bee was a palace guard as she watched me round the corner. I could have kicked myself for getting her into this mess. I had no business dealing with the likes of James. I had to drag the bags of clothes to the second floor. My legs were aching, and my back was on fire. Apartment 224 was in the middle of the complex. Women were sitting out on the stoop with babies in their laps. Music was blasting from the other ending of the ramp. Was somebody in the complex deaf? The darn TV was blasting.

I stopped in front of 224. My heart was beating so loudly I'm sure I didn't need to knock.

"Come on in the door is open, I been expecting you."

A tall heavy female was slumped down on the sofa. She had on the ugliest blond wig I have ever seen. This had to be Liz. She was as I had imagined her. She looked like she had been through the ringer a couple of time. "My name is Marie I'm."

"You are coming to my house and you don't think I know who you are Little Girl. You didn't listen when I told you to get out of this mess with James. Well, you are hooked like a catfish on a pole. When James gets through with you, you will wish you were dead."

Liz sat back on the sofa and drew a long gulf of the can of beer she was drinking.

"I said my name is Marie. I have some things for James. Is he here? I don't have all day."

"No Little Girl. That's his plan. He is going to make you wait. He left a little while ago. He said to tell you to wait. He would be right back. You might as well sit down. Standing there looking stupid ain't gone make him come back any quicker."

"Liz I have no intention of waiting for James all day. Here is the order. I am out of here." I threw the sack of clothes on the floor and turned for the door.

Two steps into the doorway there was James blocking my exit. Fear gripped me like a snake. I was on his turf. He could get rid of me right now, and no one would know the difference. He stood there smiling that evil smile. His signature brown hat tilted to the side, silk shirt half buttoned, "Hey Pretty Lady where you think you're going in such a hurry. I have to check my order before you go anywhere. Sit down."

"I assure you that everything is there James. I don't have time for any more foolishness; I am leaving."

James moved toward me and away from the door. "I have to go James now get out of my way!" I knew this would be my only chance to get away. I lunged for the front door, slipping by James. With fire in his eyes, he caught my arm and held it tight.

"I'm going let you go for now, to give you a chance to get yourself together. You will be making weekly deliveries, so you had better be calm. When you get to work Monday, you will call me.

I will have your next order ready for you. Call at noon. For every minute you are late, it will cost you."

He released his grasp on my arm as I slid to the floor. I sat there in a daze for a few seconds before I jumped up and ran through the door. The shriek of evil laughter followed me down the stairway as I leapt down the steps two at a time. At the bottom of the landing, cane in hand, purse on her shoulder, ready for battle was Cousin Bee.

"No please don't come up go back to the car, I'm on my way down!" "You alright? You look like you had a fight with the devil himself."

"It's time we got the heck out of here Cousin Bee. You deserve to know what's going on, but I am in no mood to retell all that drama.

All you can do is pray that this mess will be over soon although I have a feeling that it won't be."

"Marie I saw a tall guy with a brown hat and shirt, looking fine and sassy go up the stairs a minute ago. Is he the one that's got you in a pinch? Child, I have met a ton of them kind in my day. When they get their hooks in you, sweetheart they don't let go. What did you say his name is?"

"His name is not important. I have involved you too much already. I will figure a way out of this mess. Please don't tell Mama, you promised."

"I told you I know how to keep my mouth shut, what did you say his name is?"

I pulled out of the parking lot on two wheels. I never wanted to see this part of town as long as I lived. Cousin Bee was getting on my nerves with all these questions. It's not like she could do anything to help me. What good will it do for her to know James' name?

We rode home in silence; it was well after two when I turned off the car in the driveway. I was exhausted. All I wanted to go was go to bed. I couldn't get that voice out of my head, "Call me on Monday, and I will have the next order ready for you." How am I supposed to get another set of clothes and shoes without looking suspicious? My head was pounding. *Oh Lord, please help me!* Cousin Bee stared at me all the way home. I guess she couldn't take it anymore and she had to say something.

"Ok, you are home and safe. What is his name? I suggest you tell me, cause I will find out on my own."

"For goodness sake his name is James! James Littleton I met him at a bar a few days ago. I wish I had never gone to that bar with Cathy. Now will you leave me alone?"

I slammed the car door and stomped off toward the house. I left Cousin Bee sitting in the car. I stood in the front yard a minute trying to see what was taking her so long to get out of the car. I didn't know if she was praying or just sitting there talking to herself. At that point, I didn't care. If she wanted to sit in the car in the heat of June that was her business.

Thelma and Mama were gone when I got home; that was truly a blessing. I poured myself a glass of lemonade and sat down at the table. James' order this week was close to three hundred dollars. I knew it would be more next week. I had to call Dr. Morrison again.

I dreaded seeing that man again. Knowing that what I was doing to him was no better that what James was doing to me.

I guess Cousin Bee decided to get out the heat. I gulped down the rest of the lemonade and headed for my room. I couldn't take any more questions. I think I was asleep before my head hit the pillow.

The conversation in the kitchen woke me around 7:00. Mama, Thelma, and Cousin Bee were talking. The smell drifting into my room was heavenly. I didn't realize just how hungry I was.

I still had on my clothes from the morning. I must have looked a mess. Mama would have something smart to say, but I didn't care.

Thelma turned toward me with a smile, "Hey sleepy head, I thought you were going to sleep your whole Saturday away. Would you like for me to fix you a plate? Cousin Bee shared her spaghetti and meatball recipe with us. I'm on my second plate you don't want to miss this one."

Mama turned around and looked at me, "Marie are you feeling alright? I can't remember the last time you took a nap on a Saturday. You are usually gone doing whatever it is you do."

Cousin Bee knew I was in no mood for a fight, "Margie Marie is probably exhausted from taking me shopping this morning. I was like a kid in a candy store when I walked into that store. Poor Marie was patient and kind enough to let me take up most of her day. Marie why don't you sit down I'll fix you a big plate of spaghetti."

"Thank you, Bee. Is it Okay if I call you Bee. I think we all know you're our long lost cousin. And yes, I would love some of your famous spaghetti. Especially if you got health conscious Thelma to eat a second helping."

"Bee is my name, and you know I'm your cousin; now let's eat."

It's been so long since I had dinner with my mother and sister. I wanted to cherish every moment. I didn't want to think about James or the deliveries. I wanted to remember how happy I was at this moment.

The remainder of the weekend passed without incident. Mama, Bee and I rode to church together. Thelma was smart she rode with CJ. They left before Sunday school was over.

I got stuck with Mama who was determined to feed the entire church and anybody else that showed up. Bee pretended to enjoy all the conversations with the other women, but I could tell she was just as eager to leave as I was.

When I finally couldn't take it any longer I told Mama that I needed to get Bee home, she wasn't feeling well. I don't think Bee minded one bit that I used her name in a lie.

26

Thelma

"Thank you for going to church with me this morning CJ. You'll never know much I appreciate it. I don't want to give Mama another reason to dislike you. I made sure she saw us before we snuck out the back door. Even though we did leave a little before the service started, I don't think she minded. Ok, you have had me in suspense long enough. I am dying to know what my surprise is. You know you can give me a little hint it wouldn't hurt."

With a big smile on his face, "No way you are just going to have to wait. Believe me it will be worth it."

We continued to drive until we were outside of town. We drove down tree lined streets. I saw houses that I have only dreamed of living in one day. We drove into a neighborhood that looked like it was right out of a magazine.

We finally arrived at 1556 Appleton Lane. CJ stopped the car. He came around to my side and opened the door.

"Babe, you should have told me we were visiting someone before you showed me my surprise?"

"You always look great Thelma Rhoades, now come on I have something to show you."

"My mind was in awe. I was looking at the most beautiful house on the block. It was breathtaking. There was a white sun porch that surrounded the entrance of the house. The porch had a large Oak swing in the corner. I could visualize Mama entertaining her ladies club on a Saturday afternoon. The house was bright yellow with large windows in front. The front yard was huge. There were large trees with red and yellow roses blooming in every direction. I couldn't help myself. I wanted more than anything to go inside and explore every room.

"We were greeted at the door by an older woman with a friendly smile. "Hello, Dr. Morrison it's so good to see you again. You must be Thelma. I have heard so much about you. My name is Dorothy Wheeler."

"Hello, Ms. Wheeler I am so pleased to meet you." It was obvious that CJ knew this woman, but he hadn't mentioned a word about her to me.

Ms. Wheeler looked at CJ with a smile, "Dr. Morrison I don't believe you have told you fiancée about her surprise."

"No, I haven't had the chance yet, but I think it's time. I don't think she can take any more of this.

Thank you for coming by Ms. Wheeler I think I have everything under control from here."

Ms. Wheeler turned and gathered her things. She took my hand, "I wish you all the happiness in the world. Have a great day." Without a second thought, she was out the door.

"CJ you know I love you, and I trust you with all my heart, but if you don't tell me what is going on, I am going to strangle you."

"Ms. Wheeler is a nice woman isn't she? She was very helpful. I told her exactly what I was looking for, and she did her magic."

"CJ what are you talking about? You told her what you were looking for?" It was all beginning to make sense. I knew he had been working on something, but every time I would ask he would just blow me off.

CJ walked to the opposite end of the large living room where he held up a sign that read: WELCOME HOME. The room started to spin. I couldn't catch my breath. CJ is this our house?" Is this where we will spend the rest of our lives?"

"That's the plan, Thelma. We have enough room for all of your family as well. I made sure your mom had a porch, I know how much she likes sitting on the front porch."

"You mean this is our home? I finally have a place to call my own. I don't know how to thank you. This house is more than I could have ever hoped or dreamed of owning. But, Babe how can we afford this? You just finished your residency. Don't worry I have already secured a position with the hospital. Dad and I will be opening the practice soon. The down payment and closing cost were a gift from my family. I didn't want you to have to worry where we would live after we were married."

"So we have the keys to our house right now."

"Yes, we do."

I pulled him closer to me, as I looked deeply into his eyes, "So I think we need to christen the house and let it know how much we love it. Wouldn't you agree Dr. Morrison?"

"Well, it all depends Ms. Rhoades. What did you have in mind?"

"I think we can find something for us to lay on, for a while."

"Darling I am one step ahead of you. I have everything we need in the car."

I stood in awe and wonder as CJ went out to the car. Who would have ever thought that Thelma Rhoades, the little girl from the wrong side of the track could ever live in a house like this?

God, please let Mama be happy for me. I know she could be happy living here with me and CJ.

I watched CJ has he climbed the steps with a large picnic basket, a blanket, and a bottle of wine. Before he could place the basket on the floor, I devoured him with kisses as I removed his shirt. He broke away momentarily to spread the blanket on the floor. He took me in his arms.

The rest of the evening was pure bliss.

27

Marie

Stacy was standing at my register waiting for me. I was late, and I didn't care. There was no joy in coming to work anymore. All my energy went to making sure I had the orders right for James. Why the hell won't she leave! Just go on about your business. I didn't feel like making up a lie about why I was late.

"Good morning Marie, are you alright? You look like you haven't slept in days."

"Has all the inventory been put out on the floor? Or should I check the stock room for more boxes?" I chose to ignore her remarks about my looks. What business was it of hers anyhow?"

"No, I made sure everything was ready since you were running a little late. Okay, I'll check on you later. You have a good morning."

Thank God she's gone. As usual the store was having a sale on something. My regular customers sought me out for advice on different merchandise. I hated being in such a bad mood. I usually enjoy helping the customers find the right outfit. I hated James for what he was doing to me.

The morning was over in a flash. I logged out of my register around 11:45. It was time to make the call. The break room was crowded. There was no way I wanted to call James with all those nosy women listening to every word out of my mouth. Why on earth are all these women in the break room at this time now anyway? Is there anybody on the sales floor?

Finally, one of the phones was free. I had no choice. I had to call James now or risk being late. Dang! Why don't they leave? The receiver was in my hand.

"Ladies I need some help on the sales floor. I do believe it's time for some of you to report back to work. Marie that doesn't include you, I see you just started your lunch break."

I almost fell to the floor. Stacy appeared out of nowhere. She's never cleared the break room before.

There was something strange about this whole thing, but I didn't have time to figure it out now, it was 11:58. I was not going to be late. I needed to hear the voice on the other end of this call. The phone rang once, twice, on the third ring he answered.

"Well hello, Pretty Lady. I see you are getting a lot better with time. I guess we have an understanding.

Liz has the order all ready for you. But you and I have to get something straight. I see you brought someone with you on Saturday. I told you I have someone watching you all the time. This arrangement is between you and me. When you come to see me, you come alone. I think you understand. Now get a piece of paper and get the order from Liz. I will see you on Friday afternoon, I'll let you know where later on in the week."

"James I ain't coming down to your apartment ever again. Especially since you insist that I come alone. I hope you understand."

"I said I would see you on Friday I will let you know where." He passed the phone to Liz, who had me wait another five minutes before she gave me the order. I couldn't believe all the things James was demanding. I didn't need a calculator to see this list easily totaled over four hundred dollars. "Liz has James lost his mind! Where am I supposed?"

"I wish you would stop whining and complaining. Don't you get it? Every week the total will go up. Until you finally can't fill the order and James will make other demands."

"What are you talking about other demands?"

"I suggest you keeping filling your orders, and you won't have to find out what the other demands are. Goodbye, Little Girl."

All the items on the list were new arrivals. Not one thing was on sale.

How is it that James knows about all the new merchandise in the store?

This is crazy, James has to have someone on the inside. It has to be Cathy or Stacy. Those two witches are the only ones that could tell him about my life. Both of them know everything there is to know about the store. I can't believe they both made a fool of me. I considered Cathy, a friend. I knew she was up to something with all of her secretive behavior.

One thing for sure if the snitch is not Cathy or Stacy you can bet I will darn well find out who it is.

At least the list didn't include shoes this week. Thank goodness I wouldn't have to deal with her asking all those dumb questions like she really cares. I wonder where that witch is.

I haven't seen her all day. I know she was scheduled to work today. She's probably on another secret mission.

Whatever, Cathy is the least of my problems right now. I have to make the call to Dr. Morrison. I need five hundred dollars this week. I know he is not going to like giving up the additional money, but this arrangement will be coming to an end pretty soon.

I have to be out of the store by 6:00 today. I was not closing this place down.

I did my best to remain focused for the remainder of my shift. When I couldn't take it any longer, I clocked out at 5:50. I routed my customers over to the new girl. I'm sure she didn't mind the extra commissions.

I was on my way to the break room, when I remembered there was a phone in the corner of the store by the men's room. It would be perfect for a little privacy when I made the call to the doctor. I'm sure he had left for the day; that was fine with me. I would be happy to leave him a message. I wonder does he check his voice mail or his secretary. Either way that's his problem I needed a callback tomorrow.

I went to the rear of the store. The store was clearing out. I finally located the good doctor's number in all this junk in my purse. The phone was ringing. Why is it that the phone has to ring this many times before it goes to voice mail? Okay! Enough is enough. How many times is this phone going to ring before the voicemail picks up?

"Hello, Dr. Morrison speaking."

"Hello, Dr. Morrison. It's Marie. I didn't think you would be in this late I was prepared to leave you a message."

"Please hold one moment please, I am in the middle of something."

I had no idea what the heck he was in the middle of, but if he thinks for one minute, I am going to stay on hold in this store he has another thing coming. As a matter of fact, he has one minute and then I will be forced to drive over to that hospital and get my money.

"Marie, Marie are you still there?"

"Yes, sir I'm still here. Is everything alright? Did I catch you at a bad time, again?"

"No, you didn't catch me at a bad time. But I must tell you this is not working, you calling me at the hospital. I think we should meet at a designated spot each week. There is no need for any more calls."

"That's fine with me doc. Why don't we meet on Wednesdays someplace downtown?"

"I would rather not be seen downtown if that's Okay with you. I don't mind coming to your job. It's on my way to the hospital. You work in one of the stores away from downtown don't you? I can come by around 7:00. Wednesdays are my early days. That way I can be sure no one will see me. Marie, I hope you understand that this is not a permanent arrangement. I will only go so far with this charade."

"Well, Dr. Morrison we can discuss arrangements at a later date. For now I need five hundred dollars a week until I say different. We can meet at 7:00 in the parking lot behind the store. I'll see you Wednesday!"

The phone was dead. The dial tone was ringing in my ear. I walked out of the store, got into my car, and drove home. I was frustrated and angry. Imagine having five hundred dollars that I have to give to this fool. This arrangement is going to be over soon. I don't have the stomach for this foolishness. I hated going home in such a bad mood. That would be another reason to get into it with Mama. There was nothing worth listening to on the radio. I kept hearing James' evil voice over and over again. When I looked up I was home.

Mama and Bee were on the front porch shelling peas when I arrived. It was nice that she finally had someone in her life. I wouldn't feel so guilty when it was time for me to leave. Thelma was nowhere in sight.

I said hello and went straight to my room. I was asleep before my head hit the pillow. I'm not cut out for all this excitement.

28

The summer was coming to an end. It was already the end of September. James was becoming more and more demanding. I was putting in half of my paycheck along with the five hundred dollars a week from Dr. Morrison. My weekly visits to the doctor were becoming far from pleasant. He hated the sight of me. I really couldn't blame him. I hated what I was doing to him and what this arrangement was doing to me.

I was exhausted and at my wits end. I didn't know how much longer I would be able to keep up this arrangement with James or the doctor.

Mama and Bee were noticeably worried about the change in my behavior. I was irritable and tired all the time. I had to work all the overtime I could get at the store just to make ends meet with James' orders.

The only thing that kept me going was planning my sister's wedding. It was just two months away. Thelma finally decided on her wedding gown and the dresses for the bride maids. She chose fall colors. I think she was using all the fall colors she could find: gold, brown, orange, green and crème. I hated the dress and the colors. I tried my best to smile every time she asked me to put on that hideous orange pumpkin colored dress on.

I just know I'm going to look like a big orange pumpkin floating down the aisle. I made up my mind to make the best of the wedding since Thelma looked so happy.

Mama's attitude had not changed one bit toward the wedding or CJ. The only time I saw a hint of a smile was the day Thelma announced that she wanted to use our church for the ceremony and our pastor to perform the wedding vows.

Mama could not control herself at church. She invited everything that could walk, talk, or smile to the wedding. Thelma finally gave up the idea of a small family gathering.

One afternoon I left work early and came home. I was exhausted as usual. I worked two shifts the day before.

I hated James. I've never hated anyone in my entire life as much as I hated him and what he was doing to me. I hated even more what was happening to me.

Shortly after I arrived home, Thelma walked in from the bus. She was carrying an armload of fabrics.

"Marie I am so glad you are home. I dreaded the idea of Mama or Bee seeing me with these fabric samples."

"What on earth do you need all of that stuff for Thelma? You already have all the colors and fabric for the wedding. Please don't tell me you have something else that you are going to make me wear."

"No Marie, you're fine. The fabric samples are for something else. You know you could help me out if you have time. CJ was planning on picking me up later, but this would be the perfect opportunity to show you something very special and dear to my heart. Do you feel like taking a drive?"

"No, Thelma all I want to do is take a bath and go to bed. I am exhausted."

"Marie are you alright? You have been doing a lot of sleeping and working all these extra hours. I've told you over and over Marie that you can tell me anything. I will help you if I can."

"I'm fine Thelma. I don't need a lecture from you right now. Can we just get in the car? I'll drive you anywhere you want to go."

It was all I could do to keep my eyes open as I drove Thelma out of town. We drove for nearly an hour until we arrived in a neighborhood that I didn't even know existed.

Finally, we turned onto Appleton Lane. There were trees and flowers in every yard. At the end of the block was 1556. Thelma pointed in the direction of a huge yellow and white house with a sun porch that covered the front. I parked the car at the end of the driveway, just in case we had to make a quick getaway.

Thelma got out and signaled for me to follow her. This trip convinced me that my big sister was a little off, or she had to be up to something.

"Isn't this the most beautiful sun porch you have ever seen Marie. Do you think Mama will like sitting out here with her friends on Saturday evenings?"

"Thelma are you alright? Why on earth would Mama be sitting on some white woman's porch sipping tea? I know old lady Larson is not about to move off the plantation, so why on earth would Mama be sitting?" I stopped in mid-sentence.

Thelma's face glowed face with excitement as tears formed in the corners of her yes. I was speechless as I turned to hug my sister's neck.

"Thelma you mean this is your house? CJ brought this beautiful house for you?"

"Yes, Marie it's my house. It was a wedding gift from my wonderful fiancée. I don't know what I did to deserve all this happiness. I just pray God allows it to last."

"Will you shut up and open the door, my goodness you and Mama have cornered the market on angels and prayers. I don't think you have anything to worry about."

We spent the remainder of the day going in and out of rooms picking out colors for curtains, carpets, and wallpaper. I don't think I have ever seen Thelma this excited or happy. She told me about all her plans for the house. She wanted to move me, Mama and Bee, into the house when she married. She insisted that I pick out the bedroom that I wanted and the colors for the curtains and carpet. I didn't have the heart to tell her that I would be leaving after the wedding.

I finally had peace of mind about leaving Claxton. I knew Mama and Bee would be taken care of. I also knew she was going to scream and complain about moving out of the house, but in the end she would come to love this place as much as Thelma and CJ.

We drove home as Thelma continued telling me all the plans she and CJ had for their lives together. Even though I was happy for my sister, I had to admit I was a bit jealous. What could I have possibly done that was so horrible to deserve to be in a mess with James while Thelma gets to live the June Clever dream? Life just wasn't fair. She deserves the joy that CJ brings to her life, but God do you think you could cut me a break. I haven't been bad all my life. My life is nothing but weekly orders from James and cash pickups from Dr. Morrison; none of which I get to keep.

CJ was patiently waiting for Thelma when we arrived. It didn't make any sense at all that someone could be that gorgeous! Thelma was one lucky woman.

"Hi CJ, Thelma showed me the mansion you brought her. I am so happy for the both of you. I can't wait to see all the little Thelma's' and CJ's running around the house."

"Thanks, Marie, I'm so happy you got a chance to see the house. As for all the kids, they can't come soon enough. Marie, I know some day you will find the right guy. Someone who will love you and treat you the way you deserve. You have to give it time."

"You guys enjoy the rest of your evening." I turned and went into the house. The one thing I didn't need was love advice from CJ.

My bed and pillow were becoming my two best friends. They both greeted me with open arms. I fell asleep the minute my friends embraced me.

29

I was wide awake at 6:00 am. Not that there was anything special about today, after all it was just another delivery day. Delivering merchandise to James was now as routine as combing my hair. My head hurt at the thought of all the money I wasted on this mess with him.

He left a message at the store for me to call him on Wednesday. I hated the thought of talking to him, so I called Liz instead. She gave me an additional special order. His snitch must have told him the new line of Gators for men had arrived. He called just before we got paid on Thursday. There would be no reason I couldn't purchase the shoes.

The regular order plus the Gators brought the total to seven hundred eighty dollars. I was sick to my stomach when I threw the order in the car on Thursday afternoon when I left work. I couldn't do this any longer. My mind was made up. There would not be another delivery.

I called the apartment to confirm the drop-off time for Friday. I begged Liz to get James to move the drop off location. She said James insisted that I continue coming to the apartment even though he knew It bothered me stepping foot in that neighborhood. It didn't help one bit that I couldn't stand the sight of Liz. She made it a point to wear one of the outfits that I had to purchase every time I made a delivery to the apartment.

James wasn't giving Liz as hard a time anymore. She was finally earning her keep. All she had to do was collect the clothes, give me my next order, and, of course, keep her mouth shut. The truth of the matter is that was the only thing that made this arrangement bearable. I never had to worry about Liz talking to me when I arrived. All she ever did was take the clothes, check the order, and tell me to get the heck out of there.

I clocked out at 6:00 pm. The traffic was clear for a Friday evening. The order was in the trunk. All seven hundred and eighty dollars of it. I reminded myself that there would not be another order. Dr. Morrison was on the verge of hiring a hit man to get me off his back. That alone was reason enough to end this mess with James.

I would call him on Monday to let him know there wouldn't be a need for any more cash payouts. His secret was safe with me.

I drove over to James' apartment as usual the parking lot was littered with men and woman drinking and carousing. I hated for them to see me get out of the car with all this merchandise. I had no intention on coming here again. James would have to meet me for the final meeting at a place of my choosing. Liz as usual was watching television with the door open when I arrived.

"Come on in Little Girl you know the routine. Give me the clothes and sit your tail down till I make sure everything is here. I would offer you a can of beer, but that would be one less for me."

"I don't have a lot of time Liz could you speed this process along."

"I'm sorry you in such a hurry Little Girl, but this is the highlight of my week. I ain't about to rush through this. You know I have to give it to you Little Girl. I didn't think you would have held out this long. The other ones usually gave up. Then James has them doing other things for him."

"Liz how do you live with yourself knowing what James is doing to me and the other women."

"Oh, I guess I am supposed to feel sorry for you. Have you ever been homeless or hungry Little Girl? Have you ever had to sleep with one eye open cause you didn't want to get raped cause your *mother* left you in an abandoned apartment while she went out and did her thang. Well, Little Girl until you have lived the life me and James had to live, don't you ask me how I live with myself knowing what James is doing to you! My brother is doing what he has to do to survive. Now sit your little bony tail down. I'm going to take my good time checking your delivery. Shut up cause you know I don't like talking to you."

"I wasn't trying to upset you, Liz. I didn't know life was so hard for you and James. Life has been tough for me as well. Believe me I wasn't sleeping on a bed of roses every night. My dad left my mom when my sister and I were little. We got flooded out of the only home my mother ever knew."

"I guess you want me to feel sorry for you. At least you had a mother and a roof over your head. Now shut up I don't like thinking about that stuff."

"I know you told me to shut up, but I have to ask this last question. What will you do when James leaves? I guess you hadn't thought about him leaving. Liz you do know that James is going to leave you when he doesn't need you anymore. He is using you just like he uses everyone in his life."

"I hate talking to you Little Girl! Don't you ever say that again cause that's never going to happen. We have always been here for each other.

I take care of my big brother, and he takes care of me. Where ever he goes, I go. I'm tired of looking at you; everything is here. Here is your next order. Get the hell out of here!"

I took one last look at Liz before exiting the apartment. She sat there looking sad and pathetic. I closed the door, which I knew she hated. At this point I didn't care. The last order was in my hand. Goodness gracious! James is out of his mind. This order had to be over nine hundred dollars. To heck with this, I watched as the crumpled piece of paper sailed to the ground.

I had an audience as I walked down the stairs. They gawked and stared until I reached my car. I turned to take one last look. I knew it wouldn't do any good, but I couldn't resist saying something, "I'm praying that all of you will come to your senses and get out of this place. There is so much more to life than these apartments."

A voice from the end of the stoop chimed in, "Oh, I guess you think you better than us."

I sat down in my car, I screamed to make sure everybody heard me as I put the car in reverse, "No, I'm no better than you. I just want better."

I knew what I had to do. Bee was right. Men like James are snakes. They grab hold of you, and won't let you go. The only way to kill a snake was to outsmart it.

Lord, Liz is going to need you after I do what has to be done.

30

Liz said she was amazed I had lasted this long. Over half of my savings was gone. I was frustrated, exhausted, and miserable. Living this life was no way to live. James had to die.

I made the call to Dr. Morrison on Monday. I tried to talk to him to let him know our arrangement was at an end. He started yelled and screamed at me about calling him at work.

"I'll see you Wednesday!" The phone was dead.

It's a good thing I was in a forgiving mood. I wanted to call him back and give him a piece of my mind.

My delivery day was a week away. Only this time James wouldn't be getting his normal delivery. When I get the money from Dr. Morrison this week, it will be all mine, to do with as I please for a change.

I arrived at work around 7:15. The parking lot was usually empty at this hour. There were three police cars and the white car that Cathy usually gets in was parked at the rear entrance of the store. I parked the car and sat quietly. I had to know what was going on. The policemen were going through the large dumpster in the back. There was one officer in the dumpster he was throwing out boxes of merchandise as the other officer organized everything on the ground.

The back door opened as two police officers brought out three men in handcuffs. I couldn't believe it. These were the guys that had been working in the stock room for years. I guess I didn't know them as well as I thought. Just as I was about to get out of the car and head toward the store. The stock room door opened again. Cathy brought out another female with her head covered. I couldn't get a look at her face, but Cathy had her in handcuffs and guided her to the police car. The policemen finished loading all the merchandise from the dumpster into the back of the squad car. One by one they drove off with the suspects in the car.

I was about to burst with curiosity. I had to know why Cathy was with the police officers. We hadn't talked that much in the past weeks. It would probably be better if I asked Stacy about all the action this morning.

I clocked in and ran to my register. Stacy was nowhere in sight, which is totally unusual for her. Anytime there was something to see she would be in the mix.

I checked in other areas of the store before I went into the stock room. Standing at the rear door, just like before was Cathy, the store manager, and a detective. The situation was becoming weirder by the minute. The detective shook the floor manager's hand as he turned and walked out the door. Cathy and the floor manager turned and caught me as I exited the stock room door.

"Marie please wait. I need to talk to you. I know you have questions about what's going on."

"Cathy I don't want you to think I was eavesdropping on you. I couldn't help but wonder who are these people? Why are they here?"

"I have wanted to talk to you for months, but I couldn't say anything because I was undercover. I work for a Lost Prevention firm Marie. The store hired my firm in conjunction with the police department to stop the flow of merchandise leaving this store on a weekly basis. I couldn't risk bringing you into the middle of this."

"So you have been watching all the employees, and pretending to be my friend."

"I have been watching the employees, but I knew from the beginning that you were not a part of the thefts. The friendship part was for real. I don't usually get to make many friends on the job. I enjoyed your company, and it was nice to get a chance to go out and have fun."

"Well don't keep me in suspense. Did you get all the bad guys? I know

Stacy will be in shock when she finds out."

"Yes, we did get the bad guys, but Stacy should be getting over her shock right after they finish booking her."

"What did you say? Stacy was part of the ring of thieves?"

We believe she was the ring leader. But I believe she was working with someone else. I don't think she is smart enough to run this type of operation. From what we could tell she would give the three men in the stock room the list of merchandise to steal every week. The men would gather the merchandise and stash it in with trash along with other items in the dumpsters. Stacy would alert her boss when to make the pickup. We discovered bundles of brand new store merchandise being sold on street corners.

I have to tell you, Marie. I was a little worried about you. When you asked me to hold shoes in the stock room for you. I realized that something else was going on with you. When Stacy made a point to cover for you each time. I realized that she was trying to throw me off her trail. But Marie, I am still not convinced that you are not in some trouble. You know you can tell me. Maybe I can help?"

"Thanks for letting me know what's going on Cathy. I'm glad everything is over and done. Does that mean you won't be working in the store any longer?"

"Unfortunately, I will be moving on to another store over in Jackson. Please keep in touch. Or maybe you can visit me."

"We'll see Cathy. Take care I have to get to work."

"I was furious as I walked back to my register. How could I have been so foolish and trusted Stacy? I hope she rots in jail. I should have known, she was always asking me about my mother and my sister. I was overjoyed when I told her my sister was getting married. What did she do? She blabbed her big mouth to James. Well, Mr. James, you don't have eyes in the store anymore. You don't even have anyone to steal for you any longer. That's all the more reason for me stop these foolish deliveries.

James will be angrier than a hornets nest when he finds out that Stacy is gone. Of course, he will expect me to keep up with the deliveries. I can end this madness right now if I tell Cathy that James is the lead man in Stacy's crew, but they don't have enough evidence to convict him. You can bet Stacy is so head over heels in love with that fool that she would never give him up.

The store was a mad house with managers and police officers coming and going the remainder of the day. Stacy asked me to work a double shift today, but that was before she got the boot, there was no way that was going to happen. I didn't need to work anymore overtime hours. It was time to focus on how to get rid of James.

I clocked out and jumped in my car. I was looking forward to the drive home. The evening air smelled fresher. The river beneath the bridge seemed clearer today. I felt a sense of relief knowing there was no one in the store watching my every move.

As I reached the end of the bridge, I saw an old car coming straight toward me. The driver was driving like a maniac. This fool had to be on something. I swerved the car to the right, then to the left to avoid hitting him. I hit the gas pedal and turned into my neighborhood. The driver turned and forced me to make a sharp turn to avoid hitting him. What's the matter with this fool? He's trying to kill me. I jammed my foot on the brakes and turned to get a look at the car. A tall figure emerged from the car. He was walking toward me. My feet were stuck to the floor. I couldn't move. I didn't have time to get out of the car before the man was standing at my door. Lord help me! It's James!

"Hello Pretty Lady, I decided I would drive out to the house today to see how you were doing with all the changes going on in the store. I hope you know that nothing has changed! My guys will be back, this is only temporary. I'm expecting my delivery on Friday evening just as planned.

I know you hear me, but just in case you need further convincing." His hand was in the car. He grabbed my chin turning my head toward him. "Remember I know where you live and I have eyes everywhere."

I couldn't stand him touching me. I tried to jerk my head, "Don't you ever put your hands on me again! Now get away from my car and out of my way."

The car jerked into gear as I pulled away. James grabbed the steering wheel. "What is wrong with you James let go of my car?" The car lunged forward. James wouldn't let go.

The veins in his head and neck were bulging and pulsating. He was struggling to speak; his anger was uncontrollable, "I don't think you understand something, Pretty Lady. I run this operation, and I own you.

You will do what I say damn it!"

James had control of the steering wheel. He was trying to force me to the side of the road. I struggled to keep my foot on the gas pedal. *God help me!* My hand found the empty soda bottle in the passenger seat. The bottle burst into a thousand pieces as it landed squarely against his head. The blow stunned him enough to release the steering wheel. He fell to the ground.

I was shaking like a leaf on a tree. James was out of control. I knew he would come after my family next. I had to make my move this weekend.

When I got home, Bee was on the front porch. I wanted to go straight to my room take two aspirin and go to bed. I prayed I could stop shaking enough to get past her. I had one foot on the front porch.

"You alright Marie."

"Yes, Bee please. I can't talk right now."

"James from the apartment still giving you trouble. That snake is tightening his grip. It won't let go till it kills you. He's never going to let you go. It has to be something I can do to help you?"

Tears washed my face as I turned on my heels toward the door, "I don't know what it is you think you can do. You are just an old woman who knows nothing about me and my situation. Please leave me alone."

I slammed my bedroom door hoping that everyone understood that I didn't want to the bothered. I was suffocating. The sadness and pain of this situation was unbearable. I would have to end James' life before he took mine. I couldn't believe the words were coming out of my mouth, but there was simply no other way.

It made perfect sense. He wasn't bringing joy to anyone's life. Liz and the other girls he was pimping out would be a lot better off if he were dead. They could pick up their lives and begin again.

I know Mama owned a gun. She kept it in the chest against the wall.

It was the only thing that Daddy didn't take when he left.

I had to wait until I was alone to get the gun from Mama's room. Then I would have to figure out a way to get James away from Liz, but for now I have to deal with Dr. Morrison.

I finally dozed off into a restless sleep. Snakes of all shapes, sizes, and colors covered me. James was standing above a pit. The snakes were dragging me further into the darkness. I had to get away. You *can't have me*! I screamed in the night. I sat up in bed drenched in sweat. It was after 3:00 am. I hope I didn't wake anyone.

I was wide awake when the alarm went off. Mama and Bee were busy with breakfast when I finally staggered out of my bedroom. The look on her face told me that Bee had already told her about my attitude last night. She handed me a cup of coffee as I reached for a coffee cup in the cabinet.

"I need you to sit down; it's time you and I had a talk."

"Now is not a good time Mama. I'm already late for work, and I don't need a lecture. Bee, I'm sorry about the way I spoke to you last night."

"Marie I believe I asked you to sit down. Something is going on with you. You're not yourself. Sweetheart, we care about you. Please let us help you. Honey you know you can tell me whatever it is, I promise I will understand."

My head was pounding, and my ears were ringing. I had to get out of here. I didn't want to say something to Mama that I knew I would regret later. My hands were shaking so hard I couldn't hold the coffee cup. I backed away from the table and went toward the door. Mama and Bee were staring in amazement, "Mama don't worry about me I'll be fine. If you want to help me please keep me in your prayers."

Mama was coming toward me. I couldn't let her touch me or hug me. I knew I would break down in tears.

"Marie I pray for you every day. You have to believe that. God is with you every step of the way."

Bee managed to grab my hand before I exited the door, "Marie you need to listen to your mother. We can help you with this guy. You can't go on like this much longer. I have money, Marie. Do you need money to get this man off your back? I know that snake has a price, they all do." Mama whipped around to face Bee, "Man, what man? What are you talking about Bee? Do you know what's going on with this girl, and you been keeping it a secret?"

I grabbed my purse from the chair and ran to my car. Tears soaked my face as I drove to work. If only it were that simple to take Bee's money and pay James off. Bee's money would never be enough to satisfy James. That would only open up another can of worms.

I was even more convinced of what had to be done. James Littleton had to die. He was no longer needed by anyone.

31

D r. Morrison was waiting for me when I arrived at work. He parked in the rear of the parking lot. Someone else was in the car with him. I couldn't get a clear look at the face, but I knew it was a man. I had a feeling it wasn't good from the look Dr. Morrison had on his face.

The doctor was out of his car, and at my car before I had a chance to get out. "Good morning, Marie. I hope you have a few minutes before you have to go into work. We need to talk about a few things."

"Dr. Morrison I had a rough evening. I don't want to get into an argument with you. Would you mind if I say something before you say whatever it is you have to say?"

"No, Marie I am in charge. I would prefer to get this over and done. I have gone along with this little charade of your for a while Marie. I hoped that you would come to your senses and realize that I am not the kind of man that you can blackmail for any length of time. But it appears that you are not as sensible as I imagined, so I have decided to take matters into my hands." He reached into his jacket pocket and pulled out an envelope. "Marie here is five thousand dollars. It's enough money for you to leave Claxton and start a new life someplace else, California, Las Vegas it doesn't matter to me as long as you realize that this is your final payment. I won't put up with this arrangement any longer. I want no further contact with you regarding this matter. I hope I make myself clear." He turned to look at his car in the rear of the parking lot. "I would hate to have to take this matter to the next level."

It was all I could do to keep from laughing. My luck was changing. "Are you quite finished Dr. Morrison? Since you are in charge is it alright if I speak? When I called you the other day I was trying to tell you that your secret was safe with me. Your debt is paid in full. But since you are in charge and taking matters into your hands, I guess I would be foolish not to take your final payment, and call this arrangement to an end."

I got out the car, shook the good doctor's hand, and looked toward his car. "It was nice doing business with you. Thanks again for the money doctor. You have a great day. Tell your friend in the car I said hello."

I walked around to the back of my car and placed the envelope of money in the trunk. As I walked into work, Dr. Morrison was heading toward his car. "By the way Dr. Morrison please give my best to Mrs. Morrison and your little friend at work."

It appeared that things were beginning to look up for me. The money from the doctor was my ticket out of Claxton. Now all I had to do was take care of that unfinished business with James.

Going into work felt normal again, now that Stacy was gone. I didn't have anyone snooping around reporting my every move to James. I had to admit that I missed Cathy. After that incident with James last night, I needed someone I could trust. I'll give her time to get settled and take the drive to Jackson and say hello and hopes she forgives my behavior.

After I had finished my shift, I drove around downtown to clear my head before driving home. It was time to locate the gun and move forward with my plans for James.

I needed everyone out of the house so that I could search Mama's room. She has always kept the darn thing in the chest in the corner, with all that other junk she retained from Daddy. It would be just my luck she moved it someplace else, just when I needed it.

It was after dark when I finally got home. The lights were still on in the kitchen, Mama and Bee probably were still up talking.

I was halfway up the steps when I realized the money was still in the trunk of my car. I turned around and got the money out of the trunk. Bee must have heard the trunk close. She was on the porch before I could enter the house.

"Good evening, Marie. Are things any better with you and that fool, James?"

I didn't want to answer. I needed her to leave me alone. Please stop asking so many questions about James. I took a deep breath and tried to remain calm. It was time to convince her that everything was under control.

"I am doing much better Bee, thank you for asking. I worked out the situation with James. I made it clear that our little arrangement was over. I wanted nothing more to do with him. Please don't continue to worry about me. I know how to handle James."

"Marie, I've been around the bush a few too many times. I can tell when someone is lying to me, but I am not going to continue to bother you about the situation.

Just know that I am here when you need me. You look tired. Why don't you go in and get some rest."

"Thank you for being concerned about me, Bee. I am so glad that Mama has you in her life. It's been so long since she has had a real friend.

Good night."

I left Bee standing on the front porch when it dawned on me that I needed her out of out the house tomorrow as well.

"Bee, is Mama scheduled to work tomorrow?"

"I'm sure she is; tomorrow is no different from any other Thursday. I don't see that old woman giving her a day off in the middle of the week."

I came back out on the front porch to make sure Mama wasn't listening. "You know Bee she will never admit it, but she is getting to old to be still cleaning up that big old house. When I worked my other job, I would stop by occasionally and help her clean. My schedule simply won't permit me to help her out anymore. I remember Thursdays were her busiest day. Especially if that old witch was having guests over on the weekend. I'm sure she could use a hand if you are not busy."

"Thanks, Marie I will keep that in mind. I will speak to your mother about going in to help out. I certainly don't have anything else planned for tomorrow, and maybe we can go shopping when she gets finished.

Sleep well, Marie."

I said good night to Mama as I closed the door to my room.

Two down and one to go. I was sure Bee took the bait and would go into work with her in the morning. I wasn't worried about Thelma;

I'm sure the hospital would fall in if she didn't go to work.

I turned over and went right to sleep, without any crazy dreams. That hadn't happened in quite some time. It was nice not seeing James every time I closed my eyes.

Lord, I wish it didn't have to be this way. If there were only another way. I certainly hope you can forgive me for what I have to do. Please, if there is another way, please show me it to me.

I took a half day off work. It felt wonderful to sleep in. Mama and Bee were up bright and early preparing breakfast. Just as I thought Bee took the bait, she was going in to work with Mama. Thelma was scheduled to go in at 9:00, things were looking up.

Mama knocked on my door at 7:45 to let me know she and Bee were leaving. Thelma was stirring in the kitchen, I pretended to be asleep. I lay there in bed thinking about the thing that I had to do.

I wished I could just turn off my mind. I didn't want to think about James, or all the ugliness he had brought into my life.

The house was quiet. I hoped Thelma wouldn't decide to come and talk this early in the morning. I didn't need a sisterly conversation. Too late, I was about to drift off to sleep when there was a knock on the door. Of course she didn't wait before storming right in.

"Marie are you up? Marie, I need to talk to you."

"Well, I guess I am now Thelma. What could be so important that you have to wake me up on the only day I decide to sleep in?"

"Marie, I know it's been really good for Mama to have Bee here to talk too. But I'm worried that she will not want to come and live with me and CJ, especially if she thinks Bee won't be comfortable."

"Thelma you are going to be late for work. Don't worry about Bee and Mama. Bee will probably come and stay with you and CJ to ease Mama's fears, but I don't think she will be there for any length of time." I took my pillow and threw it at her, "Stop worrying, everything is going to be fine. You need to worry about your sister coming down the aisle in that pumpkin you have me wearing. Close the door behind you."

Twenty minutes later Thelma was gone. I jumped out of bed and ran to her room. I stopped dead in my tracks when I opened the door. The room looked like a page out of a magazine. There wasn't a thing out of place. I stood in the doorway for a moment. I had to memorize everything to make sure the room looked exactly the same when I left, or she would know I had bothered her things.

The large, oak chest sat silently in the corner, as it had for years. Mama's past life was in that chest. I had no business going through her things. I stepped back from the chest and sat down on the bed. I felt awful for what I was about to do. What if there are things in this chest that she never wanted her girls to know, things that her girls shouldn't know? I can't do this, the bed is straight. Everything looked exactly as she left it. I stood to leave. I wanted to leave, but I didn't have a choice. I needed the gun.

The rag dolls Mama collected were standing guard over her chest. I picked up the dolls and placed them on her bed in the same order as on the chest. The lid of the chest was in my hand. Just my luck it was locked. Where would she keep the key? Everything was in its place, and a place for everything. The key had to be somewhere sacred. Of course her grandmother's Bible in the corner. The key along with our baby pictures was tucked in an envelope in the back.

The key slid right into the lock. It was like walking back in time. I prayed I could move all of her belonging without her being aware. In the corner of the chest was an old photo album. I couldn't help myself I had to take a look. I assumed there were pictures of my dad, or me and Thelma.

At first, I didn't recognize anyone in the pictures other than Mama. But then I saw that flame burning on top of Bee's head in one of the pictures. I don't remember ever seeing pictures of Mama when she was a young woman she looked so pretty. She had on a long stunning black gown. Her hair was down. She could not have been over eighteen. Where was this taken? Why was Bee in most of the pictures? I continued turning the pages in the album. There was an old article from a newspaper about a house fire in Memphis. The owner of the house was Beatrice Lawrence.

Lady Bee as the article referred to her was taken to the hospital in serious condition after the fire. I folded the article back in place. I continued to turn the pages when I ran across the picture, the picture that told the entire story. Mama and a younger version of Bee together in the living room of the large house that had burned in the fire. There were four or five other women in the picture. Bee was definitely in charge. Seated in a large high back chair with her smile of authority in place. The ladies were surrounding her. They all had the same ring on their right hand. That must have been Bee's signature ring. They were all smiling except for Mama.

It wasn't all that difficult to put two and two together. My mother was a working girl in Bee's house. I was about ready for the graveyard at this point. *My dear sweet Mama* a, Oh my God I couldn't even say the words. Mama was a hooker a working girl.

It all made since. She never had anything good to say about any man, not even the pastor. I guess she had good reason to hate all men. Maybe that's why she never thought any man was good enough for her daughters.

The remainder of the pictures in the album were of Bee and Mama with different men and other women with men. I had seen more than I wanted to see. Why couldn't she be honest with us? We would have loved her anyhow.

Tears burned my cheeks as I closed the album and carefully placed it in its place. At the bottom of the chest, wrapped in a linen napkin was the gun. There were two or three loose bullets in a plastic bag.

I grabbed the bag and the bullets and placed them on the bed. I took my time and placed everything back exactly as it was. When I finished, I took a look around, the room looked like I had found it. I closed the door and went back to my room to change clothes and get to work.

I put the gun in another handbag, so it wouldn't be visible in my car. All I had to do now was get James Littleton to meet me some place other than his apartment. I had the perfect location in mind it was just a matter of getting him there.

I got dressed and rushed to my car. I crossed the bridge with every window in the car rolled down. I wanted to smell the river and feel the cool breeze wash my face. I wanted my lungs to burst with fresh air. I could finally see a way out of this mess. I would have to adjust to a new normal. James would be dead and I would be free. *Who was I kidding I would never be free again.* Nothing would ever be the same.

My thoughts shifted to the chest in Mama's room. If only I hadn't seen those pictures. I didn't need or want to know about my mother's past.

It wasn't too hard to imagine Bee as a Madame. She knows her way around men. She fingered James for a snake the minute she laid eyes on him. If only I could tell her what I have planned for James. She would never allow me to go through with it. She would do her best to fix the situation, or better yet she would try to buy him off. There is no amount of money in the world that would satisfy James Littleton. I can't allow James to hurt anymore people. There is no other way.

32

Bee

I dreaded riding to work with Margie. I knew she was still upset with me cause I hadn't told her about Marie. But what could I do? I had to get the girl to talk to me so that I could win her trust.

"It ain't no need in you being mad at me Margie for not telling you about Marie. She would have told you herself if she felt like you would listen and not judge her. But this ain't no time for you to waste time being mad at me. Believe me, Marie done got caught up with a real fool. His name is James. She took me down to his apartment a few weeks ago. She delivered a bunch of clothes and other stuff to him. I believe he has her delivering new clothes to him on a weekly basis, that's why she been so tired and working so much overtime. Well, you got anything to say, or you just gone let me keep running my mouth."

"Lady Bee, you know I love you like a mother. But you should have told me about this weeks ago. We could have been helping my baby get out of this mess."

"Okay, so you know now. What are we going to do? This snake is squeezing her pretty tight. We have to get in a hurry."

"The first thing I have to do is take care of Ms. Lena. Since I'm just finding out, I have to go into work today. After work, we will work together to get Marie out of this mess."

We parked in the rear and entered the house through the kitchen. Mrs. Larsen was already waiting for Margie when we arrived. It's amazing to me how on earth Margie went from a prostitute to a maid. But I guess when you think about it, it's not that much difference in the two. With both jobs you are waiting on people. And it's usually the people that bother you the most.

I know Margie is bursting at the seams to ask me about that fool James. But know was not the time. When things settle, the first thing I have to do is figure out a way to get Margie out of this old woman's house. She's been working for other people long enough.

"Good morning, Margie. I see you brought your friend with you this morning." She extends her hands to me like I'm supposed to bow and kiss it. I guess I do have to be nice this is Margie job for now.

"Good morning, Ms. Lena. You look mighty pretty this morning. How are you feeling?"

"I'm quite well, how are you, Bee? Thank you for coming and helping with the house today. You know Margaret is not getting any younger."

"Well, Ms. Lena Margie could probably use a little help around here. Don't you think?"

"I have asked her over and over to let me hire her someone to help her with this big old house, but she insists that she has to keep it clean the way she wants it. Bee were you able to get everything straightened out in Memphis before you moved to Claxton?"

"Well, Ms. Lena It wasn't a whole lot that I had to do. Once Margie said she was taking me out of that place it was just a matter of throwing things in a bag and telling a few people goodbye."

"You and Marie sound like you shared a special bond. You don't find friends like that every day. I'm glad you worked everything out. Margie, I'm ready for my breakfast. I'll have my usual, but would you mind bringing it upstairs. I think I'll lie back down. I didn't sleep all that well last night. Jack was up all night. His stomach was giving him problems most of the night, which means I was up as well. I guess I'm just a little tired."

Ms. Lena crept up the stair as silent as a ghost. Margie went over to get started on her breakfast. When Margie went upstairs to get Ms. Lena squared away, I went over to the stove and fixed me a big plate of bacon, eggs, and toast. I knew it wouldn't do any good to prepare anything for Margie, she would be too scared to eat anything without Ms. Lena's approval. When Margie walked in the kitchen, I was seated with a cup of coffee in hand.

"Why don't you sit down Margie, so I can answer all the questions you have running through your mind about Marie and this guy she has gotten herself involved with."

"Well, Bee I'm glad you brought it up. I was waiting for the right time. I still don't see how you could have kept something so important to yourself for so long? You know how I worry about my girls."

"That's why I didn't tell you. You worry yourself to death about your girls. Margie, the girls are grown women. They each have separate lives. You have got to let them go. Thelma is getting married in a few weeks, and you still don't talk to CJ."

"You don't understand Bee. Thelma is too young to be getting married. She just finished school."

"You know I don't want to talk about Thelma. She has a good man that loves her, and they will be just fine. We need to concentrate on how to get Marie out of this mess she has gotten herself into."

Margie stopped fiddling around in the kitchen and finally sat down in a chair at the table. "Bee I have always told the girls that there is nothing they couldn't tell me. Why would Marie confide in you and not her mother?"

"I told you that is not important. Marie is desperate for a way out of this mess. Desperate people do desperate things when they are facing a hopeless situation."

"Bee, you don't think she would do anything stupid: like end her life, do you?"

"Margie I'm not worried about Marie ending her life. It's James' life that I am worried about."

Margie sat quietly in the chair wringing her hands as tears rolled down her cheeks.

"Bee can you please help me get this house cleaned. I need to get home to help my child."

I placed my breakfast dishes in the sink and started the dish water. "Margie what did you have in mind. I told you I have asked her a thousand time to let me help her, and she continues to say no."

Margie went underneath the kitchen sink for her cleaning supplies. As she was about to exit the kitchen, she looked over her shoulder. "Bee I appreciate you telling me this, and for all you've tried to do to help my child. I don't know what I'm going to do to get her out of this mess, but one thing for sure God has already worked it out. *Just like he promised, it will all work out for my good.* I'm going to start upstairs. Do you mind dusting the first floor? I need to let Ms. Lena know that I will be leaving a little early today. I need to get home to take care of a few things."

Ms. Lena stayed in bed the rest of the day. She didn't even come down for lunch. I know Margie was worried about her. But the issue with Marie was weighing heavy on her mind. When we finished, Margie made a call to Mr. Larson. She told him Ms. Lena had been in bed all day. He told her that he would come home early to check in on her. Margie cared a lot about this old woman.

When we left, we went straight to the grocery store. A sure sign that Margie was stressed out. Cooking was her outlet. She brought enough food to feed an army.

Marie was nowhere in sight when we got home. Margie pretended she wasn't bothered. Said she was praying about what to do next.

33

Marie

Work was the last place in the world I wanted to be today. I missed Cathy more that I cared to admit. I could use a friend right now.

After I clocked in I waited for the break room to clear. I picked up the receiver to call James, but then decided it would be best if Liz broke the news to him that I wanted a change of venue to make the delivery. Our old house down by the river was the perfect place. By the time the police find his body, I would be long gone.

Liz answered the phone on the fifth ring. She does that to irritate me.

"Hello, what you want calling me this early in the morning? I was going to call you later to tell you where James wants you to deliver the order."

"That will not be necessary Liz. I'm calling you to tell you where James can pick up his delivery. Do you have a pen and paper to take down this address? Don't worry I'll spell all the words for you."

She chuckled in a spiteful manner, "You real funny Little Girl. It won't be so funny if I tell James to add a hundred dollars to your order."

"You can do whatever you please Ms. Liz, but you need to write down this address because I don't have all day. Are you ready?"

"Why can't you come to the apartment like you been doing? This place ain't good enough for you anymore?"

"Like I told your brother. I don't ever plan on coming to that apartment again. The address is 1210 Murray Lane. It's in Claxton right by the river. I'll meet him there tomorrow afternoon. Tell him not to be late?

"You know Little Girl, you got some nerve thinking you can talk to me that way. I think I will tell James it's time to raise you order. Hello, hello are you still there? No, she didn't hang up on me. You can bet this is definitely going to cost her."

I moved the phone away from my ear and let the receiver hang to the floor. I couldn't stand the sound of her voice any longer. She was still talking as I walked off. She could keep right on running her mouth. I guess she was giving me a piece of her mind. Which she obviously couldn't spare when I walked out the door.

I walked on the sales floor and greeted my first customer, one of my regulars. It felt so good to help a customer again. I looked at the new merchandise. For the first time in a long time, I can finally look and decide what I wanted for myself.

I made a couple of purchases, before leaving the store at 5:30. The gun was still on the seat where I placed it this morning. I needed time to myself; to think and make a plan. James was no fool. I couldn't underestimate him, one thing is for sure I'm sure he knows I am up to something. It probably wouldn't hurt if I took a drive to the old house just to make sure everything is in place.

I put the car in drive and headed in the direction of the old house. I wish I knew how I ended up in front of one of the most expensive hotels in Franklin. I have passed by this place a thousand time. I have never given one minutes thought about staying in a place like this. I guess I needed to rest more that I needed to go to the house. Spending a few nights away from Mama and Bee would surely do me some good. After a good nights' sleep, everything will fall into place.

The valet strolled up to the car, as I eagerly jumped out and handed him the keys. I strolled right up to the registration desk as if I had a million dollars.

"May I help you with something this evening ma'am?"

"Yes, I would like a room," I said with a smile on my face.

"Yes, ma'am. Would you please sign the book for me? How long will you be with us ma'am?"

"Let's just say for two nights for now. I'll let you know if I change my mind."

"How will you be paying for your room this evening? Do you have a credit card that you would like to use?"

"No, that won't be necessary. I'll be paying in cash." I reached into my purse for the envelope of cash that Dr. Morrison had so graciously supplied. I loved the feel of those hundred dollar bills in my hands. "Here you are sir, thank you so very much."

"Thank you, Ms. Thompson, I hope you enjoy your stay. Please let me know if there is anything I can get you?"

That was really smart not giving him my real name. I have to be careful that I don't leave a trail of any kind.

The room was on the fifth room. I stepped off the elevator and into a dream. The hallway had plush gold carpets. Room 535 was near the end of the hallway. My God! This one room was bigger than my bedroom and Thelma's together. There was a large king size bed with enough pillows to fill a palace. I ran into the bathroom.

Wow! Is that a tub or a pond? I turned on the water in the tub and poured half the bottle of bubble bath. Within minutes, bubbles had taken control of the tub. I couldn't wait to undress and step into the water. If this is the way rich people live, I was destined to be rich. Soaking in that tub was like falling on a cloud.

I soaked for an hour in the tub. The bath helped me to release the stress of the day. I didn't realize how exhausted I was. I got in bed and lay there staring at the ceiling. I thought about Mama and Bee. I would love for them to experience such luxury one time in their lives. They deserves to be treated like queens after all they have been through.

I knew they were probably worried sick about me. It was really selfish of me to be enjoying myself in this manner when Mama is out of her mind with worry. She probably has God and all his angels on alert.

Bee will probably take Mama to James and Liz's apartment. I would give anything to see Bee tangle with Liz. Liz will never tell them where her brother is. Mama will fuss, cry and pray. Bee will yell, swear, and threaten.

In the end, I will be long gone, and James will be dead.

I'll give Thelma a call at the hospital tomorrow so that they know that I am alright. The king size bed took control of my body. Within minutes, I was fast asleep.

34

Bee

Margie went straight to the kitchen when she got home. She started fixing all of Marie's favorite. I guess she thought that would make it easier for Marie to open up when she finally came home. I already knew that was a waste of time, but it gave Margie something to do to ease her mind. She started cooking and before long the kitchen looked like a cafeteria. She fixed greens, fried chicken, candied yams and was working on an all butter pound cake. It was after midnight when she sat down at the table. We sat at that table all night long and waited and waited hoping Marie would come home. We were both in a battle with sleep. Sleep was winning, but we refused to give up. I didn't think I could drink another cup of coffee when Margie got up to put on a fresh pot. When I couldn't take it any longer, I tried to convince Margie to go to bed. Still she refused to lie down.

"Margie you know Marie will be alright. She just had a few things that she had to deal fix. It won't do you any good to stay up all night worrying."

"Why don't you go ahead and lie down Bee. I just want to sit here a little while longer; maybe she will be in a later."

I know she was praying that Marie walk through that door at any minute. I had to admit I was saying a few prayers myself.

I went into the living room to lie down for just a minute, before having to get up and check on Margie again. The minute I hit that sofa, sleep grabbed me like a thief. The last thing I remember was Margie saying good night, and covering me with a blanket.

The morning sun kissed me awake. I struggled to get my legs to move. When both legs decided, they wanted to cooperate I decided to go fix a fresh pot of coffee. Margie was at the kitchen table where I left her last night. She looked so peaceful I hated to wake her. I eased over to Marie's bedroom praying that she had come home last night. Her bedroom was just as she had left it the night before. I stood there in a complete daze rubbing my forehead back and forth trying to ease a headache that was slowing creeping in. Marie where are you? I whispered softly toward heaven.

I had to get Margie to lay down. I knew she was exhausted.

"Margie, Margie wake up. You need to go and lay down. Go get some rest."

"Lady Bea, did Marie come home? Is my baby alright?"

"You get some rest I'll take care of Marie." I guided Margie to her bedroom. She was out like a light. I covered her with my blanket and closed the door.

The water was ready for coffee. But I had seen enough of this kitchen. I went out on the back porch to clear my mind. All types of possible scenarios with Marie and James were running back and forth through my head; movement from the kitchen brought me back to reality. I jumped to my feet. It had to be Marie.

"Hey Bee, how are you this morning?"

"I'm fine Thelma how are you this morning. Would you like for me to fix you some breakfast?

"No, I'm a little queasy this morning. I don't think I could keep anything down. If I get hungry later, I will grab something at work. You have a great day Bee. I hope Mama is sleeping in. She looked tired. By the way, did Marie make it home? I tried to wait up for her. It's so seldom that I get a chance to talk to my little sister."

"No, she didn't make it home. I'm sure she spent the night with a friend. You know Thelma crackers are good for that queasy feeling. Ice helps too."

I turned and walked back to the porch. I told myself, Bee; you don't have time to focus on Thelma right now. That situation will take care of itself. I have to focus on Marie.

35

James

Man, I'm tired as hell. This damn bump on my head is not helping one bit. When I get my hands on Pretty Lady, that's the last thing me or anyone else will ever call her again. I need to check this bump out. It must be bigger than I thought. Liz keeps this bathroom so darn nasty. What the hell? It looks like I have a grapefruit on my head. Well, Pretty Lady you will pay for this big time. I don't think she's getting the message. She has to be taught a lesson.

I'll give her a call before the delivery today. Her order just went up to eleven hundred dollars. There is no way in hell she can come up with that kind of money. I'll have her out on the stroll by the sundown tonight. We'll see how she does with all that smart talk when I put her with one of my roughest clients. I just need to lay down for a few more minutes. My head is killing me.

Liz has that address where I am supposed to meet her. Something about this new location just ain't right. I need to think on my feet. I'm going to get to the location a little bit early to check the place out. I hope she ain't stupid enough to have the police stake the place out. That would be deadly for her health.

What the hell time is it getting to be? Okay Its 8:00. I'll give her a call around 10:00 just to confirm everything. Almost forgot, she's off today. I guess it's time I called the house. Maybe I can even talk to dear old mom she needs to know what her sweet youngest daughter is doing.

Right now. I need my head to stop hurting. It would help if Liz weren't playing that damn TV so loud.

"Liz get the hell up and turn that TV down. I told you we don't live in a barn!"

"Why don't you close your door? I can't hear over the music from next door."

"Man, I can't wait to get the heck up out of here. I'm leaving Liz the hell behind. Anywhere would be better than here with her and those other fools. I may as well get up and make that call laying here is a total waste of time. The way my head is pounding I won't be going to sleep anytime soon.

Where in the hell did I put that number? I have it here someplace. I made sure Stacy gave me all the numbers. It's a good thing I did cause her butt is going to be in jail for a long time. I wish the hell she would quit calling me. If I didn't need to keep her on the line until she's sentenced, she would have been history a long time ago. When the trial is over; she can kiss James Littleton goodbye. I ain't spending a dime to help her out. Where the heck is that number?

"Liz I need you to get up and get me Marie's number at home. I need the number now you need to get up! Don't make me come in there. Now get up!"

Liz came through the door like an Amazon warrior, "Okay are you satisfied? Here is your number. Will you need anything else, Your Highness? It ain't my fault your head hurts all the time. I told you; you need to go to the doctor."

"I told you I will ask for your advice when I need it. Did you get those other two fools out of here bright and early like I told you?"

"Yes, I did James, but Dee Dee is not feeling well James. I think you need to take her to the doctor?"

"I ain't stopping her from going to the doctor. As long as she can fill my order and go to the doctor that's fine with me. Now will you get the hell out of my face and out of my room?"

Liz stood in the doorway with tears in her eyes, "James do you remember when we were kids. We promised to take care of each other? James, I know you are not telling me the truth about these headaches? Please let me take you to the doctor."

"You know I remember most about our childhood, Liz?"

"No, James."

"Being hungry, cold and broke all the time. I made up my mind when I got out of there; that I would never be hungry or broke again. No matter what I had to do. Now I need to you leave. I do believe I could make a little change if I put you on the stroll. Close the door behind you."

"I love you big brother, ain't nothing you can do about it."

I hate it when she reminds me of my past. Liz knows I don't like thinking about that mess we called life. Where is the phone? It's time to make that call.

Okay, old woman answer the phone, I don't like to be kept waiting.

"Hello, hello who is this?"

"Hello, may I speak with Pretty, Marie?"

"Who is this?" What do you want with Marie?"

"Well, what I want is to speak with Marie. We have some business we need to discuss."

"Well Mr. Business Man, my name is Lady Bee. I am Marie's cousin. She told me all about you. Not that it was that much to say."

"Lady Bee or whatever the hell your name is. I need to talk to Marie about her delivery today. The total went up a hundred dollars."

"I see. Where is Marie supposed to make this delivery to today?"

"You sound like you a pretty sharp old woman. Why don't you figure it out? You tell Marie if she knows what's good for her she better not be late. She can bring that extra hundred dollars in cash."

"Just how long do you plan on keeping this arrangement with Marie?"

"As long as I need to. I have no plans to make any changes. I own Marie, from head to toe. It's just a matter of time before I have her working for me full time."

"You pretty sure of yourself aren't you. I think it's about time someone taught you a lesson Business Man. I'm just the woman to do it."

"Bring it on old woman. I can find something for you to do too. For now tell Marie she better be on time this afternoon."

"You know James it ain't nothing I hate worse than a snake. They ain't good for nothing. I'll give you one chance to do the right thing and leave Marie alone. Name your price. I'll get you your money today."

"Oh, so you do know my name. I don't need your money old woman. I got plenty of money, and besides I got Marie and the money. But thanks for letting me know that when I get tired of Marie your money is always an option. Who is that yelling in the background?"

"Bee who is that on the phone? Is that Marie?" Margie struggled from the bedroom, still half asleep.

"Okay, so Marie ain't at home? I guess you can fill dear old mom in on our conversation. I'm tired of talking to you. You don't have anything I need." I slammed the phone down in her ear, hoping I had done major damage.

Okay, Pretty Lady where are you this early in the morning? You are probably at the new location. It's time for me to make my move.

Where are my pills? I think I'm taking too many of these things in a day. It not like they're doing any good. For once Liz may be right, I do need to check out these headaches. I'll go into the free clinic one day next week. I hate giving doctors any of my hard earned money.

"Liz I'm getting ready to go. I need you to call me when those two fools get back with their orders. I want you to tell them to wait here for me until I get back. It's time I had a little chat with those two. I'm sick of them laying up here every day. I need them out on the stroll."

"James why do you have to be like that. I already told you that Dee Dee wasn't feeling well. Maybe if you gave her a day off it would make her feel better."

"Okay, since you so worried about the two of them; you can tell Dee Dee that she can stay home tomorrow, and you will take her place. That works just fine for me. Need you to get out the house. You have a closet full of new outfits, I suggest you find one that goes with the stroll. Now get up and close this door. I'm going to take care of Pretty Lady."

36

Bee

"Margie I need you to hurry up and get dressed. We got to get a move on." "Who was that on the phone Bee? Was it Marie? Did she call after I went to sleep? Lord we still haven't heard from her? I think we need to call the police. Something may have happened to her."

"We don't have no time to call the police Margie. It takes them forever to take care of anything. Marie needs our help right now. That was James on the phone. He's the one that is giving Marie the trouble. He is a snake of the worse sort. We're going down to his apartment to see if it's anybody we can talk to that can help us out."

"Bee you do believe Marie is alright don't you?"

"I believe she is alright. She has no idea who she is dealing with, so we need to hurry." Margie turned to walk back to her bedroom.

"Oh my God!"

"What is it?"

"I was too tired to notice last night, but Marie has been in my room. It had to be her Thelma would have mentioned if she borrowed something."

"How do you know she's been in your room, Margie? We don't have time for this."

"Isabell and Angelique, my rag dolls are facing each other. That's not how I left them. Bee, she must have gone in the chest. Suppose she looked at the album and the other things. She knows all about me. That's why she didn't come home. She hates me for lying to her all these years." "Margie we got bigger things to worry about. Get dressed and let's find Marie or you will never get the chance to explain anything to your daughters."

"Bee she went in the chest. She put the key back in the Bible. I have to know did she look at the album." Margie yelled from the bedroom

"Margie removed the rag dolls from the chest."

My heart went out to her. She spent most of her life shielding her girls from her past, and it was all coming back to bite her. She sat down on her bed.

"Bee she saw the album. She even read the old article about the fire. How will I ever explain all of this to her. I have to make her understand. Bee."

"We don't have time for this now Margie. Marie could be in big trouble."

"Bee the gun and the bullets are gone."

"Are you sure, maybe you put them in a different place."

"No, I always keep the gun under lock and key in this chest. It's the only thing that my ex-husband didn't take when he left me for that other woman."

"Margie we do not have time to waste. She is planning on killing that fool if we don't get to him first. If you aren't ready to leave in fifth teen minutes. I will drive myself."

"We have already had this conversation, Bee. You don't know how to drive. I don't remember you taking any driving lesson since you have been living here."

"You'd be amazed at what an old woman can do once she has her mind made up."

I went back into the living room to grab my purse. My gun was under the corner of the sofa. It might take two people to get rid of this snake.

"Margie your time is up. Let's roll."

"Bee do you know where this guy lives?"

"Marie took me to his place a few weeks ago. She was making one of her deliveries. It's over in Franklin. The neighborhood reminded me of Memphis. Believe me it ain't nothing you and me haven't seen before."

"We drove over the bridge in silence. I could tell Margie was praying. I wouldn't be surprised if a whole legion of angels weren't already posted outside the apartment when we get there.

We drove by the store where Marie works. We both wanted desperately for her car to be in the parking lot, but it was nowhere in sight. "Margie quit worrying. She is going to be fine. She has handled this fool for months without our help. She is a smart girl. She's just tired and desperate. That's a horrible position to find yourself in."

We arrived at James' apartment complex around 11:00. His car was nowhere in sight.

I remembered that Marie went up the stairs to the second floor, but I had no idea what apartment she went too.

"Do you remember the apartment number, Bee?"

"No, I don't but we'll find it. *I know you still praying.* Come on I do know it's on the second floor."

Lord, this would be a good time for you to help me find this apartment. There's a TV on up here. Come on Margie! I remember hearing that TV blasting the last time I was here. "I know where we are going. The same TV was blasting in the background when James called this morning."

The noise from the TV was coming from the fourth apartment. The door was already open, but I decided to knock anyhow.

"Who is it? Whatever you are selling I don't want any. And I don't need you to pray for me today either."

"Ma'am I am looking for a guy named James. Do you happen to know him?"

"What if I do? What do you want with him? I can tell you right now, you are not his type." Liz got up from the sofa and walked toward the door.

"That's good to know. I'm certain he is nothing I would want myself. Do you know where he is or not?"

"Why you come here looking for my brother?"

"So James is your brother." Margie pushed me out of the way and burst through the doorway.

"You don't understand. I am trying to find my daughter. I believe she may be with your brother, or maybe they are planning to meet up later."

"Oh, you must be the Little Girl's mother. Well, your little girl has a delivery with James today. That's all I have to say about that. Now I need both of you to get out of my apartment before I call the police."

"What did you say your name was?"

"I don't believe I said anything, but since you asked its Liz. Now I need you to do me a favor and leave. James don't like folks all in his business."

"Liz we are very worried about Marie. She didn't come home last night. Please tell me if you know where my daughter is." Tears ran down Margie's face as she pleaded with this fool. I eased Margie aside.

"Liz we don't have time to waste with you. From the looks of you. James don't give a darn about you either. I'm sure it would be nice to have some money of your own.

So I'm going to make this simple. I can give you a thousand dollars if you tell us where Marie is making the delivery today."

"James does take care of me for your information old woman. Just like I take care of him. We got each other's back. You ain't planning on hurting him are you? Cause James is all, I got. I tried to tell your Little Girl that James was not the kind of man you wanted to get tangled up with, but she didn't listen. When will I get my money if I help you?"

"I got it right here in my purse. All you have to do is tell Marie's mother where the delivery is going to be today."

"I don't trust you anymore that you trust me. *Show me the money.*"

Margie was about to faint from all the excitement. "Lady Bee do you have that kind of money to give to her? I promise I will pay you back every penny."

"Margie I need you to go back to the car and wait for me. I'll be right down when I take care of this business with Liz."

"I would like to stay Bee. I have to know where Marie is."

"Wait outside on the stoop. I promise this won't take long." Margie turned slowly and headed for the porch.

"Liz please…"

"You can go, Margie, I told you I got this." Margie closed the door as she exited.

"Alright, Liz. I don't have time to play with you. Your brother is crazy as hell, and I think you know that. I need that address now!"

"Oh, so you in a hurry now. Well, let me tell you how this is going to go down. I ain't giving you the address until you promise me that I can go along for the ride. I have to make sure you and the angel mother don't do anything to my brother. I want half of my money now. The other half when we get to the location. Do I make myself clear?"

"Yea you real clear. I think you better get that address. We need to get a move on." I opened my purse, got out my wallet, and counted five one hundred dollar bills into Liz's hand. Now give me the address. We need to go."

"I have to go and make myself pretty. I don't get out of this apartment very often. James prefers that I stay and watch over things. The address is on the coffee table. I'll be ready in a few minutes."

"I'm leaving in five minutes, child it's going to take more than makeup to help you." The address was on the table. It looked familiar. Oh my God! It's Margie's old house on Murray Ln. I'm not ready for Margie to go down there yet. I still have work to do to get my plan in place. Why on earth did Marie have to choose that house as the drop off location? Marie what have you gone and done. I wasn't expecting anyone down at the old house until I finished fixing it up. I need a little more time. I want Margie to be comfortable knowing that she will not have to go and live with Thelma and her new husband. It's too late to worry about any of that now.

I guess Margie had to find out sooner or later what I've been up to while she was at work. "Alright, your five minutes are up! I'm leaving.

Liz came out of the bedroom looking worse than she did when she went in.

Margie was patiently waiting when we came outside.

"Bee are we going to get my child? Why are we taking her with us?"

"Don't worry Margie. I have everything under control. Get in the car.

I think we need to hurry."

37

Marie and James

I slept like a dream for a few hours in spite of what I had to do today. I stared at the ceiling until I couldn't take it anymore. It was killing me that Mama and Bee probably worried about me all night.

The room service menu was on the night stand. I've always wanted to order room service in a fancy hotel. I can afford to order anything I want off the menu thanks to Dr. Morrison, but food wasn't really want I wanted. I needed this to be over. I knew I shouldn't hate James, but under the circumstances I think God would understand.

I couldn't turn off my mind. I had to be at the house by 2:00. James should be there by 4:00, but I know he's coming early. He thinks he's going to get the jump on me. Have I got news for him?

I wish there were another way to get out of this mess with him. Why couldn't he just be reasonable and let me go. Why did he have to be so darn greedy? Why did he have to ruin so many lives? I hated to think what this would do to Liz. What on earth is she going to do without her big brother?

I can think about that now. I got out of bed and went over to the chair by the window. I missed Mama, Thelma, even Bee. The chair worked its magic on me. Sleep was waiting for me as I dozed off comfortably in the chair.

The complimentary wake-up call came at 7:00. I thought about ordering room service but I couldn't imagine eating anything right now. My nerves were getting the best of me. The mini bar was stocked with plenty of alcoholic beverages. I thought maybe I could mix up something to take the edge off. I took a small bottle of whiskey from the table.

Hey, Pretty Lady, can I buy you a drink? James! What the heck! Why the hell am I hearing his voice? It felt like I was back in the night club. He was smiling that sly evil smile that pulled me in. I slammed the bottle down on the counter. Another bubble bath would be great.

I was in the tub with bubbles up to my neck. The water felt great. I could have stayed here all day. I never wanted to leave, but I knew if I soaked any longer I would look like a prune, besides the bath wasn't doing anything for my nerves. There had to be something on TV. Nothing else was helping. I felt like a lion in a cage back and forth. The voice in my head kept said it's time to go.

I need to talk to my sister. Thelma will reassure Mama that I'm alright. It was after ten. I'm sure she was at work, where else would she be? I guess I should check at home first just in case. Please let Mama have left already. Please, Thelma be at home; please answer. The phone just kept on ringing. She's gone. I can't leave a voice mail.

"Hello, hello is anyone there?"

"Thelma is that you? It's so good to hear your voice I was praying that Mama didn't answer the phone."

"Marie is that you? Are you alright? We have been worried sick about you. Why didn't you come home last night? I worked a double when I got home Mama was asleep. Bee told me they hadn't heard from you. Marie that is very irresponsible of you. You could have at least called to check in with us."

"Well, if you are finished giving me a piece of your mind. I am trying to tell you that I'm alright. I needed some time alone, to clear my head. Thelma, I have something that I have to take care of today.

I don't want you to worry about me. When Mama and Bee get, home tell them I'm fine. I'll be home as soon as I can." I hated lying to her.

"Marie you're scaring me. Please tell me where you are? CJ and I will come and get you. What's going on? What is this thing you have to do? Who are you with Marie? Is it the same guy that's been giving you trouble?

Marie, please listen to me. You are way in over your head. Please let me help you!"

"I'll be fine Thelma. Don't worry about me. You just take care of that gorgeous doctor that loves you with all his heart. You are one lucky woman Thelma. I know I haven't always been there for you, but it wasn't because I don't love you. You have been the best big sister any girl could imagine. Thelma, I have to go. I want you to promise me that you will be happy, have lots of kids, and live the life that you and CJ want.

Thelma, there are some things that you don't know about Mama. Promise me you won't judge her when she gets around to telling you. Mama did the best she could raising us. Everything she did or said to us is because she loved us. Don't worry she's fine, just try to be understanding when she decides to talk to you about it. I have to run. Luv you girl."

Everything was set. It was time to check out of the hotel. I hated leaving this place. It was as if I belonged here. Why do I have to check out? I certainly can't go back home like everything is normal after I eliminate James. I have to have someplace to hide out for a few days. I may as well stay over till Sunday.

I went downstairs to the lobby and secured my room for one more night. When I got back to the room, I unwrapped Mama's gun. It was much heavier than I imagined. I've never touched a gun in my entire life. I hope I have the nerve to do what has to be done. Maybe James will see how serious I am and leave me alone after he sees the gun. I stood in front of the mirror and pointed. My hands were shaking, and my palms were sweating. How on earth am I ever going to pull this off? James will probably take one look at me and laugh. *You can do this Marie. There is no other way.*

There was no use waiting around in the hotel. I may as well get over to the house and get things ready for James.

The lobby was packed with new guests as I walked to the parking lot. I prayed no one saw me leaving. I drove through downtown past the store. Cars were everywhere as usual. I hadn't given any thought to what I would do about my job after ending things with James. I kept driving I couldn't think about that now.

I got to the old neighborhood at 1:30. Everything looked as it did after the flood. Time had stood still. The end of the main road that led to the neighborhood was up ahead. Murray Lane was right before the last street. I have driven this road hundreds of times. This is where Murray Lane was supposed to be. But everything was different. This certainly is not the way we left this place. There wasn't a sign of the flood. It was like somebody had changed the set in a movie. New trees covered the sidewalks. There was even a street light in the middle of the block.

Our old house greeted me as I turned the corner. But it wasn't *our old house*. I couldn't believe my eyes. Our house was painted a bright yellow with white shutters all around. The front porch with its new paint job had a huge swing in one corner. Mama's dream had come true. The front yard was beautiful with flowers and rose bushes all around. I parked the car and walked around to the side of the house and into the backyard. Oh my God! Mama's clothes line were in place again! They were ready, and waiting for a fresh load of laundry.

We could never get Mama to buy a dryer. All she would say is; *I don't need a dryer the good. The Lord gave me one years ago.* Mama would love this house. I hope the new owner loves it as much as she did. I guess the city took over the place when no one returned.

Both doors to the house were locked. I tried the windows on the either side of the house. Thank goodness the workers left the last window open. I climbed through the window into a large bedroom. The smell from the new hardwood floors waffled throughout the house. Every room had a new ceiling fan and new fixtures in the bathrooms.

The men were still working in the kitchen. The wiring for the new appliances was being installed. I wonder why they aren't working today. I looked around the house. I needed someplace to hide. There was a new closet in the hallway. Perfect! I'll hide in here and wait for James. I placed the gun and my purse on the floor and rushed back to my car.

It was 2:00. I had to get the car out of sight before James arrived. I drove down to the end of the street and parked the car behind the last house close to the levee. Suddenly, panic gripped me. What if James sees me running in the middle of the street? The neighborhood was completely deserted. It would be months before someone found my body. Run Marie!

I reached the side of the house; I climbed through the window. I raced into the kitchen and unlocked the back door. With any luck, he'll think the workers left it open.

It was hot and muggy outside. I would have killed for a bottle of water. I was hot, tired, and sweaty. I really should have eaten breakfast. My stomach needed something to do. James would be here any minute. I hated the idea of waiting for him. I felt like a stalker as I closed the door to the closet and waited for my victim.

James

It's time to get over to the house. Pretty Lady is expecting me at four. I need to get there before she does to check the place out. She probably already there, waiting for me. I wonder why she chose that part of town, anyhow. Ain't nothing down there but the river and a few run down shacks left standing after the flood? It has to be something special about that place. Whatever it's as good a place as any to do what has to be done. She's out on the stroll by sun down this evening. I don't have anybody to watch her in the store, so it's time Pretty Lady got a taste of the streets.

I better drive by the store just to make sure she didn't go into work. Damn, I hate that fool Stacy had to go and get caught, she messed up a good thang. She going to pay for this when she gets out. I'm losing money, cause she can't handle her business. No, looks like Marie didn't come in to work today.

It's hot as hell out here. She got me driving down to this swamp. I hate coming down to this part of Claxton. It reminds me of that hell hole where I grew up in. What the heck could she have in mind for me down here?

Okay, I'm supposed to be on Murray Lane. This place is pitiful. The city should have condemned this mess right after the flood. Murray Lane is a couple of blocks away. From the looks of things, somebody had mercy on this hell hole and decided to try and fix a few of these shacks up.

I wonder where she is. I know she's here waiting for me. Ain't no way she's going let me get here first? This mess has *setup* written all over it. Alright, Ms. Pretty Lady let's get this show on the road. Whatever you got planned for me, it ain't gone work. There is the house 1210. I can play this game too.

James and Marie

Time seemed to stand still. Sweat ran down my back in buckets. I heard the car pull up, the car door slammed. It was 2:30 on the dot. I knew I couldn't trust him to come on time. I got the gun off the floor. I gripped it in my hand. Oh my, God I forgot to load the bullets. There wasn't enough light in the closet to see. Please, God, show me what to do. There were three bullets in the bag. I took out all three. They were very little. I felt the barrel of the gun. I turned it around and managed to open the chamber.

The bullets were in my hand. James was surveying the house. Hurry Marie, you don't have much time. I had one bullet in the chamber. Darn it! I dropped one on the floor. Please, Lord, let me get this last bullet in the chamber. The gun was ready. I needed to step out of the closet; if only my hands would stop shaking and my feet start moving.

I watched James as he surveyed the perimeter of the house. He stepped on the front porch and tried opening the front door. He pushed and pulled on the windows on the porch as well. He moved from the porch to the side of the house. I could shoot myself for not remembering to lock the window when I came through. I needed him to come through the back door.

He tried the first window then the second. He was finally at the third window. He opened it with ease and stepped right in. James was in the house with me. I was sure he heard the pounding of my heart from the closet. I needed him to come a little closer, just a few feet past the door. I didn't want to look him in the eye when I ended his life. He looked around the kitchen, like a lion searching for its prey. He walked past the closet. Now was my chance. Move Marie!

The closet door opened. James was standing in front of me as I pointed the gun in his face.

"Hey, Pretty Lady. What the hell you think you gone do with that gun. Oh, I guess you were planning on shooting me. Put that damn thing down before I get mad."

"I'm warning you, James. Stay away from me. This gun is loaded, and I will shoot you." All I had to do was pull the trigger. I aimed the gun at his heart. In a split second James would be over. "You made me do things that I never imagined doing James."

"I don't want to hear that crap. If you gone kill me get it over with." He took off his hat and threw it on the floor. He unbuttoned the sleeves on his shirt and rolled them up. Okay, shoot me. I'm standing right here in front of you.

Suddenly, he took both of his hands and began rubbing the side of his head as he spoke. "I'm going to give you one more chance to drop that gun. Then I'm going to take it and show you what a real man is. You see Ms. Pretty Lady I own you. I have owned you from the first time I laid eyes on you. I owned you when you smiled and accepted my drink. Now, you do what I say." Why was he rubbing his head? Something was terribly wrong with James. He staggered backward and tried to maintain his balance, he was in a great deal of pain, "I'm tired of telling you the same damn thang! Now give me that gun."

I had to get out of the closet. I took one step. The bullet I dropped rolled under my foot. When I looked down James lunged for the gun. We both had a death grip on the handle. I refused to let go. James grabbed my hands. He was pulling my fingers away from the handle. He managed to get the gun away from me. I had to get the gun back. I pushed him as hard as I could turning and jumping on his back. We were on the floor. He tried to throw me off. The gun slipped from his hands as we rolled around on the floor. "I'm going to kill you! I'm go- ing to kill you."

Something was happening to James. I rose from the floor, kicked the gun aside, and scampered to the corner. James tumbled over. His body retracted into a fetal position.

"My hea--d my-my hea--d." His eyes were closed.

"What's the matter with you, James? I'm not stupid. It ain't a darn thing wrong with you. I'm not falling for the oldest trick in the book." I stared at this curled up body on the floor. I couldn't help but feel sorry for him. I crawled over to his body on the floor. "James what's wrong with you?"

"He--lp me my head. Pleeese"

His left arm lay close to his body. His fingers were curled tightly in a fist. Oh my God. Something is wrong with you. You can't die on me. Please hang on. I have to get you some help. God, what do I do?

"Marie, Marie. Are you in there?"

"Mama, Mama I'm in here. Mama, Bee, and Liz burst through the back door. I ran into Mama's arm like a kindergartner on the first day of school. She pulled me into her arms and hugged me so tight I couldn't breathe. That was the best feeling in the world. I never wanted her to let me go.

Liz nearly knocked Bee and Mama down as she ran toward James' lifeless body on the floor. "James, James wake up James I'm here. Please don't die. I need you big brother." Tears ran down her face as she held his body in her arms. "Why are you standing here? You have to help him. What did you do to him?"

"I didn't do anything to him, Liz. We were wrestling for the gun when suddenly he grabbed his head and fell to the floor."

Bee walked over and looked at James. "Well, his brain's about through cooking. From the looks of things, he has had his self a stroke. Looks like it's a pretty bad one too. By the time the ambulance gets him to the hospital, it will be a full-blown stroke."

"This is all your fault. Are you going to stand there and just let my brother die? I'll tell the police that you caused this. I'll tell them that you lured him all the way out here to kill him. I promise when I get through with you, you will wish you had never met my brother."

Liz had fire in her eyes. "Well Liz, for your information I already wish I had never met your brother. If I hadn't met your brother, I wouldn't be in this mess. You wait just a minute Liz, I am not completely heartless. James is sick, but I believe he will be fine. I'll go and get help."

Mama knelt on the floor by James' lifeless body. She was talking to every angel in heaven.

Bee stood in the doorway, as she looked at Liz frantically trying to revive her brother. "Wait a minute Marie before you go running off. We have to get a few things straight. Liz, I hope you are listening. I know you are worried about your brother.

You do realize that we will be forced to tell our side of the story when the police get here. It wasn't like your brother drove all the way out here to help plant flowers in the neighborhood."

"What are you running your mouth about old woman? My brother could be dying. Marie, I said go get help!"

"Marie don't you move. Like I said if you plan on telling the police about Marie. You must be planning on seeing your brother in a prison hospital; cause that's where he will be when I get through telling my version of the story. Like you pointed out I am an old woman, so they are more likely to believe me. The ball is in our court. We can get your brother to the hospital. I know of a wonderful facility in Memphis that he can recuperate in. Of course, I'll make arrangements for them to take you too if you want to go. James will be eligible for government assistance. I'll help with your expenses for a year; then you're on your own. Which one will it be Liz, the home or the prison hospital?"

Liz was beside herself with grief as she looked away from her brother. "I couldn't care less about that Little Girl. Please help my brother."

"Alright, Marie you can go. Looks like he should be well done about now."

The ambulance along with the police arrived about twenty minutes later. Liz didn't say a word as Bee told the police that she was fixing up the houses in this neighborhood for the underprivileged. She asked me to show the house to Liz and her brother. In the middle of showing the house, James started complaining about his head hurting.

They took him to the hospital in Franklin. CJ and his father happened to be on call when we arrived. CJ told us later on that he had suffered a massive stroke. More than likely he would be paralyzed on his left side. Liz was devastated. She told CJ that James had been complaining of headaches for months, but she couldn't get him to go to the doctor.

Mama and Bee went home. I went back to the hotel for one last night of luxury. I didn't have the energy to answer all the questions that I knew Mama and Thelma would have. Mama complained about me leaving again, but Bee explained that I needed this time alone to get my head on straight.

Bee told Mama she had been working on the houses in the old neighborhood right after she arrived. I didn't have anything else to do when everyone else left for work. I wanted to repay you for all you, and the girls have given me. Your house will be ready just before the wedding. One other thing you won't have to worry about me being underfoot any longer.

I bought the house next door and two other houses on the block. I'm going to get Dot and bring her back to live with me. Mama was speechless with excitement. She was finally going back home.

38

Liz

I hate hospital. Everything is always final when they get you in here. But it's going to be different this time. James is going to get better. I don't have a way to maintain the business while you're sick James, but I can take care of you. Please down be upset with me. I don't know what else to do. Dee and Lisa and your other girls are just as lost as I am. Your hands feel so cold and clammy, maybe this lotion will help. .I hate you're sick like this, but at least I get to talk to you.

James when are you going to wake up? You have been in the hospital for two weeks. They finally got you stabilized. I have been worried out of my mind. Why didn't you listen when I told you to take care of those headaches? The doctors says you are going to be paralyzed on your left side for the rest of your life. But, we will show them. You will walk again! James Littleton, you aint going out like this. I'm going to take care of you and get you back up on your feet. We have some unfinished business to attend too. For now, we will go and live in this home. She's going to pay for me for a year. That's just enough time to get everything in order. Then we will take care of Ms. Bee, that Little Girl and the angel mother too.

I don't know what I would do without you big brother. It's so horrible to see you in this condition. Damn! It's all that Little Girl's fault. If she would have stopped delivering the orders, then you could have put her on the street, and that would have been the end of that. She had to go and mess everything up for us.

It won't be long James, hang in there. We leave for Memphis at the end of the week. The doctors have done all they can do for you here. Don't worry about

Dee Dee and Lisa. That old woman had a house down by the river where you got hurt. She is going to let them stay there for as long as they need to or at least until they can get up on their feet. That's the least she could do; it is her fault that we are homeless. I guess it is for the best. James, Dee Dee went and got herself knocked up. She probably thought you would feel sorry for her and cut down on her orders when you found out she was pregnant. How stupid can she be? The only person you care about is me. Right, big brother. Please try and talk to me James. I know it's hard, but please try to say something. I need to hear your voice. I am so scared without you. Lord why didn't he listen.

James

I wish you would get the hell out of my room. I'm so tired of your whining and crying about how much we mean to each other. I've been awake for days. I don't feel like saying anything to you. I don't give a damn that you are scared. I'm the one laying in this hospital bed paralyzed. You are right about one thing I will walk again.

I will take care of Pretty Lady and especially Ms. Bee, but for now I have to get better. Then I will take care of all of them. I can just see Marie smiling from ear to ear. She thinks she has seen the last of James Littleton. I have to put up with Liz and her whining until I get better, but as soon as I'm on my feet there will be hell to pay. They better not put us in a room together when we get to this home. I don't want to look at her any more than I have too.

I don't know why in the hell she thinks I am worried about Lisa or Dee Dee. It ain't like I didn't know she was knocked up. It's my baby. Damn, I'm going to miss that money. I had a nice little couple already lined up to buy the brat. That's alright I'll get the money on the next round. For now I need to use all my strength to get better. I ain't finished with you yet Pretty Lady. I have something special planned for you and me.

39

Marie

James was finally over. But I didn't take any pleasure in the way things turned out. Mama finally asked me about the things that I saw in the chest in her room. She said it was time that she told me about her past. I thought about it for a while. I didn't see the point in dragging up all that old history. I knew what I needed to know about my Mama, and that was that she was always there when I needed her. As for telling Thelma I told Mama not to worry about that now. Thelma would be fine not knowing.

James and Liz went to the home in Memphis in late October. CJ told Liz that James could quite possibly regain partial use of his body with rest and rehabilitation. It didn't seem to bother Liz as long as she still had her brother.

It was a little over two weeks before Thelma's wedding. Bee asked me and Mama to take her back to Memphis to pick up her old friend, Dot. Mama didn't want to go back to Memphis, so I agree to drive Bee. I was thrilled to get out of Claxton, even if it was for only a short time.

When we arrived in Memphis, we went straight to the home. Bee had called the home and told them to help gather Ms. Dot's things. She was waiting for us under the skylight in the lobby.

Bee was overjoyed to see her old friend. "Hey, old woman are you ready to hit the road. It's time to get up out of here. That is if the man in the skylight says it Okay."

Dot's smile filled the room when she saw Bee, "Bee I'm so glad to see you. I told them that you would be coming back to get me. The man in the skylight told me that you had a few situations that you had to clear up. I don't know how to thank you. I didn't want to die here among strangers. I have packed all my things I am ready to hit the road."

I asked the nurse if all the arrangements were taken care of for James and Liz's arrival. The nurse assured me that they were ready to make them as comfortable as possible. Liz would be in Dot's old room, and James would be right across the hall. Bee asked me to drive her by an address in her old neighborhood. When we parked, she asked me and Dot to wait in the car for her. She got out of the car and walked along the sidewalk. She stopped for a while and smiled. When she came back to the car, she told me to get the car going and don't waste any time getting her out of Memphis. Her life was in Claxton with her family.

Mama moved back into the old house. She was waiting on the front porch when I dropped Bee and Dot off at their new home next door. She told them to put their things up and come and eat dinner. She had enough food for an army.

40

Everything was going well. I should have been excited and looking forward to the future. I received a promotion at the store, I even had my own office. I had sales associates answering to me. I didn't want any part of the drama that came along with James, but I missed having someone special in my life. I guess that will all come in time. Look at the time I better get back on the sales floor. Darn it, it's the phone again. Probably somebody calling in sick, I don't need this today.

"Wilson's Fine Clothing Marie speaking how may I help you?"

"Hello, may I speak to Marie Rhoades?"

"Cathy is that you? It's so good to hear your voice again. I was so worried that you wouldn't return my call after the way I treated you before you left."

"Marie I was so worried about you. I prayed I would hear from you again. I knew you were going through a rough time. I wish you would have allowed me to help you. How are things now? You did get rid of that fool, James. I know he was the source of most of your grief."

"Cathy I don't know how to begin. How much time do you have?"

"Girl I am so glad to hear from you. I will make time for this conversation. Besides ain't nothing going on with me that's more important than catching up with you. I'm all ears."

"You were right about James. He was the source of all my stress. Cathy, James was blackmailing me. He threatened to hurt Mama and

Thelma. Stacy was his snitch in the store. You know she was helping the men steal from the stock room. She told him everything about me. I was terrified. I didn't know what to do. So I went along with him. Stacy will be serving time, for her crimes. James never bothered to help get her out of jail or anything else for that matter."

"Girl are you serious? You didn't have any money. What were you giving him?"

"I am so embarrassed by what James had me doing. To make a long story short. I had to purchase clothing and shoes from the store every week. I would deliver the items to James on the weekends, or whenever he snapped his fingers."

"Marie I know you didn't come into a big inheritance, so where were you getting all this money?"

"I was blackmailing my sister's father-in-law, Dr. Morrison."

"Wait a minute girl, let me close this door and sit down. Now repeat what you just said."

"You heard me, Cathy. I'm not proud of what I had to do, but James gave me no choice. I caught the doctor in a compromising position, and I took advantage of him. I was no better than James. I told myself that I was doing what had to be done. That's the only way I could live with myself. At least now that's all over."

"Marie where is James?"

"He is where he will never bother me or anyone else. James suffered a massive stroke, Cathy. He and his crazy sister, Liz are in a retirement home in Memphis, compliments of Bee."

"Girl do I even want to hear how that situation came to be?"

"Let's just say everything worked out for the best." There is a silver lining to this story. Do you remember me talking about Bee?"

"Yes, that's your mother's relative from back in the day who came to live with you guys."

"Cathy, Bee was an angel in disguise. She purchased our old house and fixed it up. It looks amazing. She even bought the remaining houses on the street. She fixed up the house next door for herself. When we delivered James and Liz to the home, she brought back Dot, her best friend from in the retirement home. The two of them are as happy as can be in the old neighborhood. She has been restoring the other houses to benefit women and children that have fallen on hard times."

"Marie that is awesome, but where did that leave you? Did you move back to the old neighborhood with your mom and Bee?"

"Girl you will not believe this. The best news of all. I finally have my very own place! Yes, no Mama, no Thelma, and no Bee. I have my place that I can call my own. I thought Mama would have a stroke when I told her that I wasn't going with her, but Bee convinced her that it was time to let me live my life."

"It is so good to hear you laugh again. Okay, so is there a new man in your life?"

"I know I am ready for someone new, but I don't know if it's time to consider that option. I am so busy with the store. Are you ready for this? I am the floor manager, but I guess you already knew that.

The manager told me that you put in a good word for me before you left. I can't tell you how much I appreciate your help. When I got the promotion, I figured it was time for me to get off my duff and get back to school. I'm taking a couple of classes at a time. I'm enjoying being exposed to new things."

"I am so happy for you. Okay, I've heard about everybody except Thelma. How was the wedding?"

"Oh my God! Cathy, the wedding was beautiful. Thelma looked radiant in her wedding gown. I don't need to tell you, that the groom was fine as wine. That man looked so good I wanted to jump in front of Thelma and marry him myself. Mama cried the entire ceremony. I think she is finally excepting CJ, at least I hope she is.

The wedding would have been perfect if Mama hadn't invited that old hag, Mrs. Larson. That old woman makes my blood boil. She knows that I can't stand her. I think she does things to spite me. Anyhow, I managed to avoid her for most of the ceremony. Then Mama invited her to be in the wedding pictures. She had the nerve to say that old woman was like family. So here we are, the entire family at the altar about to take pictures. That old witch just had to go and spoil my good mood by commenting on my dress. I think everyone in town knew I hated that orange pumpkin dress that Thelma made me wear. Mrs. Larson waited right until we were taking pictures, she blurted out, "Marie you look so lovely dear. You look just like a Halloween pumpkin." It a good thing Bee caught my arm, or that old woman would have been history."

"Marie I think you are going to have just accept that Mrs. Larson is family. Your mother cares a lot about her."

"Oh my goodness Cathy, I have to get back out on the floor. I have to get by Thelma's to drop off some more maternity clothes. I can't believe I'm saying maternity and Thelma in the same sentence. I'm going to be an aunt. Can you believe it? The baby will be here next summer. Mama is going to be a grandmother. She is already sewing and buying things for the grandbaby."

"How exciting Marie. You'll have someone to spoil."

"It took Mama a minute to accept the fact that Thelma was pregnant when she got married, but then the grandmother fever hit her, and she was alright. I have to admit I was pretty shocked myself. My sister had sex before her wedding. Lord will heaven ever recover?"

"Marie I have to go. Please don't be a stranger. Since you have your place, maybe I can spend the weekend with you and you can come and visit me sometimes. I'm going to be at this store for a while. They're having an even bigger problem than we had at Wilson's."

"Okay, Cathy I'll let you go. We'll talk this weekend. I am so glad to have my friend back. Take care."

It was good talking to Cathy. I didn't realize how much I missed her. Look at the time. I've got to get out of here. I still have to check my box. Then I am gone.

I don't understand why employees can't tell you they are going to be out. Instead, they leave stupid notes in the box for me to find later.

I walked around the corner to the break room. Here we go again. The room cleared the instant I hit the door. I know the feeling. No one wants to be asked to stay over. My box was full of messages. As usual Theresa will be late, and Taylor is not coming in. Oh my, God, it's another note from Dr. Morrison. I wish he would quit trying to contact me. I told him his secret was safe with me. I guess I will have to talk to him to get him off my back. I stuffed the notes in my purse and clocked out. I couldn't wait to get to my car. It was days like this I just wanted to go home and sleep.

When I reached the car, it was only 5:30. Too early to go to Thelma's. I didn't want to be stuck there all evening looking at baby books.

Oh, darn where is my cell phone? I finally decide to get a phone, that I can never keep up with it. I must have dropped it in my purse. Where is it? Keep ringing, please keep ringing. Oh my, God, it's him again. Hello, Dr. Morrison. Yes, I've gotten your messages. I would have to be blind to ignore them. I don't understand why you keep trying to contact me. I told you your secret was safe with me. You don't have a thing to worry. If there is nothing more for us to discuss; you take care.

"Not so fast Marie. You know we hardly got a chance to get to know one another. I called to see how you were doing. You know we are practically family now. I was wondering if you would like to meet me someplace quiet for a drink. I would like to know if you got that problem you were dealing with corrected. I hope you know that I am willing to be of service if you need me."

"Why that's very kind of you Dr. Morrison, but that won't be necessary. I have that problem under control. Maybe we can have that drink some other time. I have lots of studying to do, and I am meeting my sister later on."

"You don't have to call me Dr. Morrison, Marie. Why don't you call me Charles?"

"Is that what the lady on the couch in your office calls you? I think I'll stick with Dr. Morrison."

"You know Marie it doesn't hurt to have someone like me in your corner. You'll find that I am very helpful in certain situations. Just like I was when you were in that bad place a few months ago. I spoke with Liz; you remember Liz James' sister. I got a chance to talk to her quite a bit when I was treating her brother. She told me all about the arrangement that you had with her brother. Don't worry she asked me not to say anything because Bee would be taking care of her brother. But I would hate to let it slip to your dear sweet sister, Thelma what you were doing to me.

So, when you get ready to have that drink, you give me a call. I can hardly wait."

"Well, Dr. Morrison don't hold your breath. I couldn't care less what Liz told you; it's her word against mine. I would think that you wouldn't want my dear sweet sister and her lovely husband to know who you were spending your break time with. Besides, Dr. Morrison you have a lovely wife. Why don't you try taking her out for a drink sometimes? I'm sure she would appreciate getting out of the house. You take care now."

My cell phone felt dirty as I put it back in my purse. Where is my tissue, I need to wipe my ear. I don't want any part of that conversation to linger. I can't stand a dirty old man. Don't know when he has it good. I think I'll give Thelma a call. I can drop off those clothes on Saturday. I need to call Bee. I can't wait to tell her about this new snake that's trying to crawl around in my garden. We need to get ready for this one.

Other Books by
Denise Montgomery

The Blessing is an action-packed thrill ride that will keep you on the edge of your seat from beginning to end.

Emily Holmes grew up in a dysfunctional family. Her father and mother treated her as if she didn't exist. Finally, Emily gets the courage to run away. She landed in Arizona where she meets Jeff, the man of her dreams. Will Emily's dream last? Emily now faces the prospect of having to return to Arkansas where the nightmare began?

Farmer Brown and Lady Madelyn, the Children's Story is a delightful tale of a couple whose one desire is to have children of their own. Farmer Brown and Lady Madelyn are not very bright, so Farmer Brown decides to pay a visit to Wise Old Owl to see if he can provide some assistance with getting children on the farm. The loving couple soon realize that Wise Old Owl has plans of his own.

That's not how the story ends. Farmer Brown and Lady Madelyn have many more adventures to explore before they realize their dream of having a family.